"Now you better get on over to the Redstones' place before Grace thinks you stood her up."

"Stood her up?"

"You won her basket at the box social—you're her date."

"For the square dance?"

"For everything." Before Cole had a chance to ask Candy to clarify that cryptic response, she marched to the door, grumbling. "The last thing a woman needs is a guy who won't step up to the plate and do the right thing."

The words had continued to cycle through Cole's mind on his way to the parking lot.

He *had* done the right thing.

It was the reason he'd left Mirror Lake.

And Grace.

Books by Kathryn Springer

KATHRYN SPRINGER

is a lifelong Wisconsin resident. Growing up in a "newspaper" family, she spent long hours as a child plunking out stories on her mother's typewriter and hasn't stopped writing since. She loves to write inspirational romance because it allows her to combine her faith in God with her love of a happy ending.

Making His Way Home
Kathryn Springer

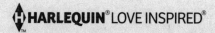

HARLEQUIN® LOVE INSPIRED®

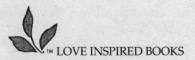

™ LOVE INSPIRED BOOKS

ISBN-13: 978-0-373-87806-2

MAKING HIS WAY HOME

www.LoveInspiredBooks.com

Printed in U.S.A.

In his heart a man plans his course,
but the Lord determines his steps.
—*Proverbs* 16:9

To Char

My friend who drives two hours to see me
when I need a sanity break (and brings lunch!)
and laughs at all the right places in my manuscripts.
You're the reason there will always be a
"Faye McAllister" in every story I write. Love you!

Chapter One

"The dress is adorable, Grace! I knew that shade of yellow would look perfect on you."

Grace Eversea summoned a smile, trying to match Kate Nichols's enthusiasm while she maneuvered her ankle-length skirt—and six inches of petticoat—through the narrow gap between the sofa and the coffee table.

Add a bonnet and a pair of button-up shoes, and people just might think she'd stepped down from one of the sepia-toned portraits hanging on the wall of the historical museum.

But then again, Grace acknowledged ruefully, that was kind of the point.

It had been Kate's idea that everyone who volunteered to help with Mirror Lake's 125th birthday celebration should dress for the part in clothing authentic to that time period.

Something Grace hadn't found out until *after* she'd agreed to act as the official tour guide for the event, transporting people to unique historical landmarks and other points of interest scattered throughout the area. In a horse-drawn wagon.

Which posed a problem that apparently only Grace could see.

"I'm still not sure how I'm supposed to sit down while I'm wearing this…bustle." *And breathe in this corset.* "I think every article of clothing they wore in 1887 was designed to pinch, itch or constrict."

At the same time.

"That could explain why none of the women in those old photographs we found were smiling." Kate chuckled as she reached for the garment bag draped over the back of a rocking chair. "I better get back to the café. Mayor Dodd wants to go over some last-minute details before the opening ceremony tomorrow. You're welcome to join us."

"Thanks, but I think I'll—" *change clothes!* "—take B.C. for a dry run. I'm not sure how long it will take to complete the whole circle. We have to make five stops—"

"Six," her friend interrupted cheerfully.

Grace blinked. "Six?"

"That's the other reason I stopped by." Kate's clover-green eyes sparkled with excitement. "I sent the letter over a month ago but didn't mention it because I didn't want to get your hopes up. But then he called yesterday, out of the blue, and gave us permission to add the property to the tour...."

"You lost me." Grace jumped in when her friend paused to take a breath. "Who called? *What* are we adding to the tour?"

"Sloan Merrick's place."

Grace's breath snagged in her lungs, and this time she couldn't blame it on the corset. "I didn't think that property was still in the family."

"I wasn't sure, either. That's why I went to the courthouse and did a little investigating." Kate grinned. "Apparently Sloan left the house and land to his oldest grandson when he died."

An image rose in Grace's mind, swift and clear, almost as if it had been lingering just below the surface of her memories, waiting for permission to appear.

Shaggy hair the color of a midnight sky. Crooked smile. Eyes the rich, deep green of a fresh cedar bough.

Cole.

"Right." Kate's eyes widened and Grace realized she'd said the name out loud. "Anyway, he apologized for not getting back to me sooner. His only stipulation for letting people tour the property is that we check the cabin first to make sure it's safe. Isn't that great?"

"Great," Grace echoed.

"I'm surprised you remember Cole," Kate went on. "I don't think he lived in Mirror Lake very long."

"A summer," Grace murmured.

And yes, she remembered.

A girl didn't forget the first time she'd fallen in love.

Or the first time her heart had been broken.

But she didn't tell Kate that Cole Merrick had been responsible for both.

"One hour and twenty-six minutes, B.C."

The old draft horse stomped a platter-size hoof and tossed an aggravated look at Grace.

Okay, so maybe she hadn't added in the ten minutes the wagon had been parked in front of the gravel road leading up to Sloan Merrick's house.

Grace closed her eyes.

What was *wrong* with her?

Her yard bordered the Merrick property. She'd driven past this exact spot hundreds—no, *thousands*—of times on her way to work and hadn't thought about Cole.

But over the past few hours, memories had begun to pop up like dandelions. Grace no sooner yanked one out than another one immediately took its place.

She couldn't blame Kate. No one, not her parents or even her closest friends, knew that she and Cole had formed an unexpected bond when his family had moved in with Sloan the summer before her senior year of high school. At seventeen, Grace had been shy and bookish; Cole grieving his father's death and angry at the world in general.

They'd come face-to-face one afternoon in Grace's favorite spot—a boulder roughly the size and shape of a hammock that jutted out over the lake. Anxious to finish the book tucked under her arm, Grace had stumbled upon a boy trying to light one on fire. An English text, which made it even worse because that happened to be Grace's favorite subject.

She'd rescued the book and ordered him to leave. Not only had Cole refused, but he'd also returned the next day. And the next. After several days of ignoring each other, a tentative friendship had begun to take root. And as the weeks went by, it had blossomed into something more.

They'd talked about their families. Their fears.

Their future.

That's why Cole's abrupt departure had come as such a shock. In the days and weeks that followed, Grace waited for the phone to ring. Checked the mailbox every day. Twice. In time, she'd come to the realization that he hadn't felt the same way about her.

By the time her senior year of high school ended, Grace had stopped waiting for him. Not *thinking* about Cole had been a little more challenging, but she had managed it.

Most of the time.

"Come on, B.C. Let's get this over with and go home." Grace clicked her tongue and the mare obediently plodded forward, right between two rusty No Trespassing signs hammered to the oak trees that flanked the gravel driveway.

The two-story brick house wasn't visible from the road, so she hadn't realized how neglected the property had become since Sloan's death four and a half years ago. The man had been meticulous in maintaining the spacious grounds, but weeds had taken over the raised vegetable gardens and branches from a recent storm littered the yard.

The original homestead, a rustic cabin with a crumbling layer of white chinking between the logs, sat at the edge of a small pond garnished with cattails. Lilac bushes scented the air with a heady, soul-stirring fragrance that rivaled the perfume counter of an exclusive boutique.

No wonder Kate had wanted to add the Merrick place to the tour. Even in its neglected state, there was something appealing about the structure. A simplicity that reflected a time when life had been the same way.

Grace hopped down from the wide plank seat and looped B.C.'s reins around the weathered pole of an old clothesline. She waded through the tall grass and circled the cabin, on the lookout for potential hazards to curious children and petticoats.

As she rounded the corner, her gaze drifted to a narrow opening between two poplar trees. And even though it wasn't part of her scheduled tour, Grace was drawn down a path that only existed in her memory.

As the wooded area opened to a small clearing along the shoreline, she stopped dead in her tracks.

A man stood on the rock, hands in his pockets, facing the lake.

Apparently she wasn't the only one who ignored the No Trespassing signs.

Mayor Dodd had warned everyone to prepare for an influx of visitors. Not only had people in the community invited their family and friends to attend the celebration, but Grace's friend, Jenna, had also mentioned it in the weekly column she wrote for the online edition of *Twin City Trends* magazine.

As if he sensed Grace's presence, the stranger turned around to face her, his face shadowed under the brim of a ball cap.

"Sorry." She took a step back. "I didn't realize anyone was here—"

"Grace?"

Her breath stuck in her throat.

Either her mind was playing tricks on her...or Cole Merrick was back in Mirror Lake.

Twelve years disappeared in the blink of an eye.

Cole was seventeen years old again, about to torch a textbook and sprinkle the ashes over the water, when a girl had stumbled into view. Eyes the color of dark chocolate had widened with astonishment when she'd spotted him.

Almost identical to the expression Cole saw on her face now.

Well, he was feeling a little shell-shocked, too, by this unexpected blast from the past.

Grace Eversea. The last person Cole had expected to see. He automatically took a step toward her.

Grace took another step back.

Cole frowned. He hadn't changed *that* much over the years. A few crow's feet fanning out from his eyes—ones he held Bettina and Travis and Sean, his twin brothers, directly responsible for—but other than that...no tattoos. No piercings. The reflection in the mirror remained pretty much the same.

"It's me." He yanked off his cap. "Cole."

"I know."

I know?

Those two words might have made Cole feel a little better. If Grace hadn't tossed a quick look over her shoulder like she was searching for an escape route.

"It's...been a long time." *Because there's nothing like stating the obvious, is there, buddy?*

"Yes, it has." Grace finally smiled, but it wasn't the one

Cole remembered. The one that had made him feel like he could conquer the world. This one was distant. Polite. "I didn't expect to see you here."

It sounded almost like an accusation.

"Kate wrote to me," Cole explained. "About Mirror Lake's birthday celebration."

And if everything went the way he hoped, in twenty-four hours he would be celebrating something else. Phase two of the expansion project for Painted Skies, his private air charter service.

"She mentioned that. Today." Grace sighed. And glanced over her shoulder again.

Cole took advantage of the momentary silence to study her. At seventeen, Grace had cared more about books than shoes. Other girls their age knew how to flirt; Grace knew how to listen. She'd taught him how to skip rocks and hunt for literary symbolism buried in obscure passages of Shakespeare. A failing grade following his father's death had sentenced Cole to six weeks of summer school, and Grace had saved him from a D in English Lit.

Who was he kidding?

She'd saved him from a lot of things.

Cole had never known anyone quite like her.

But if the wary expression on Grace's face was anything to go by, she didn't feel the same way. The conversation was beginning to feel like an awkward blind date instead of an unexpected reunion between two people who had once been friends.

Close friends.

In fact…Grace happened to be standing in the exact spot where Cole had kissed her for the first time. Right underneath that silver birch…

He heard her quick intake of breath and yanked his wayward thoughts back in line.

Grace pivoted away from him. "It was…nice…to see you again, but I have to get back."

"Hold on." The words slipped out before Cole could stop them. "I'll walk with you."

He hopped down from the rock and caught up to Grace as she reached the clearing. Her figure was still as slender as the reeds that hemmed the shoreline, but faded Levi's hugged curves that hadn't been there in high school.

They fell into step together, but Grace kept her gaze fixed straight ahead. The mane of glossy, sable brown hair was pulled back into a low ponytail at the nape of Grace's neck, giving Cole an unobstructed view of her delicate profile.

Her steps quickened as the house came into view, as if she couldn't wait to be on her way.

Cole, on the other hand, suddenly wanted to know more about her.

"Would you like to come inside for a few minutes?"

Grace looked shocked by the impulsive invitation, and Cole mentally smacked himself upside the head. Grace wasn't the teenaged girl who'd turned his world upside down—and his heart inside out.

Not to mention there was probably someone who would be tempted to punch his lights out for asking.

"I can't. I have to get B.C. home," she murmured. "She gets cranky if she doesn't get her oats at a certain time."

For the first time, Cole noticed the enormous draft horse hitched to an old-fashioned buckboard.

The mare's head swung around, and she whinnied a greeting.

Cole grinned.

At least someone looked happy to see him.

Chapter Two

Grace had no choice but to follow as Cole strode over to the wagon.

"Hey, Buttercup," he crooned, knuckling the mare's wide velvety nose.

B.C.'s ears twitched in response to the husky rumble of Cole's voice and Grace's heart responded with a traitorous twitch of its own.

"I can't believe you remember her name," she muttered.

"It's pretty hard to forget a two-thousand-pound horse named Buttercup."

But apparently, Grace thought, it wasn't hard to forget other things. Like plans. And promises.

She fumbled with a strap on the mare's harness in an attempt to avoid eye contact with the man whose presence had tipped her world off its axis.

For the first time, she noticed a black midsize SUV parked on the other side of the house. If she hadn't been so distracted by her thoughts, she would have realized someone else was on the property.

But what was Cole *doing* in Mirror Lake?

Grace had never considered the possibility that Kate's letter would not only gain permission for her to lead tours of the Merrick property, but also result in a visit from the owner of the property himself.

But here he was, standing less than three feet away from her. It felt almost surreal.

After Cole had left town without a word, Grace had played dozens of different scenarios in her mind, rehearsing what she would say if their paths ever crossed again.

She hadn't realized that she would find it difficult to say anything at all. Or that Cole would be more attractive at twenty-nine than he'd been at seventeen.

His lanky teenaged frame had shot up another inch or two and filled out. He was still lean in the hips, but his shoulders were broader, his arms more muscular. The unruly strands of ink-black hair that had once brushed the top of his collar had been cropped short. Taken one by one, Cole's features could almost have been described as ordinary. Deep-set green eyes. Strong cheekbones. Angular jaw. But added together, they packed quite a punch.

The fact that she could hardly breathe was proof.

"How many miles does she get to the gallon?" he asked.

Grace refused to respond to Cole's teasing smile. "We thought the historical tour would be more fun if we used an authentic mode of transportation."

"We?"

"I'm on the planning committee."

"I didn't realize you were one of the people who'd volunteered to help with the celebration this weekend," Cole said slowly.

"I'm the only one with a horse and wagon." Grace untied the reins, a not-so-subtle hint she was ready to leave. "B.C. only comes out of retirement for special occasions now, though, like the Fourth of July parade and Reflection Days in September. The kids love her."

"So you'll be leading the tours?" Cole seemed as determined to continue their conversation as she was to end it.

"A journey back in time." Grace had come up with the name during a brainstorming session with the planning committee and the irony wasn't lost on her now.

She didn't *want* to journey back in time. Not if it meant facing Cole Merrick again.

"So you came back for the weekend?" He rested a tanned forearm on the side of the wagon. "Or do you spend your summers here?"

"I don't know what you…" The air emptied out of Grace's lungs, making it impossible to finish the thought.

Cole assumed she'd returned for the celebration.

But why wouldn't he? She'd confided in him that summer. Trusted him with her dreams.

With her heart.

"I'm not visiting. I live here."

"In Mirror Lake?" Cole struggled to hide his surprise. As far as he knew, Grace had never planned to make the town her permanent home.

"That's right." She wedged the toe of her cowboy boot inside the spoke of the wagon wheel and swung onto the seat before Cole could offer his assistance. "My parents moved to Boston to be closer to my sister, Ruth, and her family a few years ago. They bring my two nephews back for a visit every summer.

"Mom claims it's to give the boys a taste of country living, but she pulls weeds in the flower beds all day and Dad cuts enough firewood to last all winter. I think they're the ones who need to spend some time in the outdoors."

So, not only had Grace made Mirror Lake her home, but she still lived next door.

Had she fallen in love with one of the locals and decided

to stay? Cole's gaze dropped to her left hand. No wedding band or engagement ring.

He couldn't believe it. Were all the men in town blind, deaf and dumb? Or just dumb?

"Why did you decide to stay?" Cole couldn't prevent the words from slipping out.

"I love it here."

Was it his imagination, or had she placed a slight emphasis on the word "I"?

"What do you do? For a living?" Cole knew the sluggish economy had hit the northern Wisconsin counties particularly hard, but Mirror Lake had been struggling for years. He figured the only thing that had kept the town going was an equal mix of love and loyalty, along with a generous dash of stubbornness, in the hearts of the people who called it home.

"I'm a social worker."

That surprised Cole, too. "I thought for sure you'd be teaching English Lit at some fancy prep school."

Grace looked away. "Plans change."

Cole couldn't argue with that. And sometimes they were simply put on hold, waiting for the right opportunity.

"It was nice of you to let us add the cabin to our tour," Grace said after a moment, so politely that once again, Cole was reminded that she'd changed, too. "Kate asked me to stop over tonight and make sure there were no safety issues."

Cole glanced at the cabin. The sun had dissolved into a strip of clouds on the horizon and shadows funneled through the trees and crept into the yard, shrouding the small structure in darkness. "Are there? I haven't had a chance to look around yet."

"The grass is pretty tall, but I didn't see anything that could cause an injury. And the cabin appears sound."

"No…snakes?" He tried to suppress a shudder.

"No snakes." Grace's unexpected smile, the first genuine one he'd seen, sent Cole's heart crashing against his rib cage.

She was obviously remembering the afternoon they'd explored the tiny cabin and disturbed a pine snake dozing in an old chair. Cole had mistaken it for a coil of rope—until he swept it onto the floor. The thing had glided over his feet on its way to find another hiding place, but Cole had beat it to the door, leaving Grace behind in tears.

Because she'd been laughing so hard.

Truth be told, Cole was beginning to remember a lot of things about the summer he'd met Grace.

But it was the future he needed to focus on.

After he'd discovered Kate's letter—misfiled in a desk drawer, thanks to Bettina, his absentminded younger sister—Cole had contacted Sullivan and Sullivan, the only law office in Mirror Lake. Not only had the attorney recognized his name, but he'd also claimed he had a copy of Sloan's will and a key to the house—for Cole.

Until that moment, Cole hadn't truly believed his grandfather had left him an inheritance. He'd assumed the house and land, along with all of Sloan's personal possessions, had gone up for sale after his death.

Shaken, Cole had asked the lawyer why he hadn't been told about his grandfather's wishes. Sullivan had hemmed and hawed a bit before explaining that Sloan had set a condition—that Cole not be told about the property unless he returned to Mirror Lake on his own.

Cole didn't believe in coincidences, but he did believe in divine intervention.

This is your time, his secretary, Iola, had said right before Cole had left for Mirror Lake.

His time hadn't been his own since he was seventeen. But now that his mother had remarried and his younger siblings were starting their own lives, maybe he could finally believe it was true.

And all he had to do to make his dream a reality was to sell the piece of land that had been in the Merrick family for five generations.

"I'm sorry, but Sully won't be back in the office until Monday."

Cole stared at the receptionist—and apparently the other half of Sullivan and Sullivan—in disbelief. Candy Sullivan, a bleach blonde in her mid-fifties, had pointed to a chair by the window when he'd walked into the law office. Then she'd spent the next fifteen minutes chatting on the phone while she painted each fingernail a shade of red that matched the fire hydrant on the curb outside.

Fortunately, her conversation had come to an end about sixty seconds before Cole's patience.

"I picked up the key from Mr. Sullivan when I got into town yesterday. He didn't say anything about going away for the weekend."

"Yesterday Sully didn't know that Mayor Dodd was going to ask him to judge the square dance competition." Candy pursed her lips and blew a stream of air on her pinky finger. "He needs a few hours to get ready, so he skipped out early. Matilda Fletcher, she's the head of the historical society, found him the cutest pair of red suspenders—"

"You mean he's still in town?"

Penciled-in eyebrows hitched together like boxcars over the narrow track of Candy's nose. "Where else would he be, honey? A town only turns one hundred and twenty-five years old…" A brief pause. "Once."

Cole pulled in a breath and held it, trying to cap off his rising frustration. He'd promised Iola he would be back by the end of the day.

His secretary's husband, Virgil, had taken Cole's place in the cockpit for the flying lessons Cole had scheduled, but he preferred to be on the ground now, taking care of the shop. A job that had belonged to Cole before he'd bought out the business from Cap Hudson, the flight school's previous owner.

"Do you know where I can find him?"

"He's probably at the park right about now. I have to get over there myself." Candy dropped the tiny brush back into the bottle and aimed a pointed look at the clock.

"You wouldn't happen to know the name of a local Realtor, would you?"

"There's only one. Sissy Perkins."

"Where is her office located?"

"A block off Main. Right behind the bank."

"Thanks—"

"But Sissy isn't working today, either."

"The square dance competition?"

Candy Sullivan's shield against sarcasm had to be as thick as her bronze foundation because she smiled at him. "The box social. It starts at eleven, by the pavilion."

Cole glanced at his watch. If he hurried, he might have a few minutes to talk to both his grandfather's attorney and the Realtor.

Or see Grace again.

He shook away the thought and another one immediately took its place....

Grace sitting on the rock, her bare toes drawing lazy circles in the water while she listened to him recite a passage from his English text. Splashing him if he dared to grumble.

But the Grace he'd encountered the evening before wasn't the one he remembered. *That* Grace wouldn't have been in such a hurry to get away from him.

Cole felt a stab of regret for the way things had turned out. He'd thought about Grace over the years. Pictured her standing in a sunlit classroom against a chalkboard backdrop, the classics fanned out on her desk like a buffet. Each book a sample of a new literary adventure she would encourage reluctant students to try.

He'd never imagined she would become a social worker and continue living in her childhood home. She was the one who'd challenged him to pursue his dreams.

Plans change, she'd said.

But what had changed? Her circumstances? Her goals? She'd told him *what* she was doing, but not why.

Because it's none of your business, Cole reminded himself.

And right now, his business was somewhere in the park.

He waited at the corner for a brightly painted ice-cream truck to lumber past before crossing Main Street.

From the looks of it, half the town had already gathered in front of the pavilion. Cole stalked toward the makeshift stage set up in the shade of a towering maple, dodging kids and dogs and several people who looked like extras on the set of *Little House on the Prairie.*

He paused to look around, trying to find Marty Sullivan's face in the crowd.

"I think the auction is about to start," he heard someone say. "Let's get closer to the stage. I can't see what I'm bidding on from way back here."

"Just don't bid on the one with the pink ribbon tied around the handle. That one's mine."

"It's Grace Eversea's basket, ain't it?"

Cole's head jerked around at the name. He eased around the trunk of the nearest tree so he could eavesdrop—*see*—better.

Two guys close to his age stood several yards away. One of them was as tall and skinny as a fly rod, with shaggy blond hair and a full beard. The other a businessman of some kind, pale and clean-cut with a smile as tight as the garish purple tie knotted around his neck.

"What if it is?" Purple Tie sounded a wee bit defensive.

"Good luck with that," Shaggy scoffed.

"You're just bitter because Grace wouldn't go to the fireworks with you last Fourth of July."

"How many times have *you* struck out?" Shaggy shot back.

"Not as many as you."

Cole almost smiled. He wasn't sure why the guy was *bragging* about it.

"And you think winning her basket is going to make Grace forget the reason she turns down all the guys who ask her out?"

"I know it will. Women love this kind of attention. When I outbid everyone else, she'll be flattered—"

"And grateful."

His friend flashed a sly grin. "You got it."

Cole couldn't believe it. If he had his way, neither one of them would spend five minutes in Grace's company. They didn't deserve her.

"I've got twenty dollars." Purple Tie tapped his back pocket. "Do you think it'll go for more than that?"

"If it does, I've got five I can lend you."

"Great. Then I'm in."

Cole dug his wallet from his back pocket and thumbed through the contents as the bidding started.

A slow smile spread across his face.

So was he.

Chapter Three

Grace nibbled on the tip of her fingernail as the mayor's wife delivered a picnic basket to another smiling couple.

The box social was the 1887 equivalent of a blind date, something she'd managed to avoid in spite of the efforts of well-meaning friends and coworkers. So why had she actually *volunteered* to participate?

Probably because it had sounded like a fun way to kick off the celebration. But that was before *her* basket was the one the men would be bidding on.

"We're down to the last two, gentlemen." Mayor Dodd's gaze swept over the crowd as he held up a wicker hamper lined with pink-and-white checked gingham. "And I have to say, something in here smells mighty delicious."

"Is that one yours?" her friend Abby O'Halloran whispered.

Grace could only nod as the butterflies in her stomach took flight.

"Who will give me five dollars for this basket?" Mayor Dodd bellowed, his voice carrying through the park without the aid of a microphone. "I see your hand back there, mister."

Grace didn't dare turn around and see who'd placed the first bid. Abby and Kate, however, had no qualms.

"I can't see who's bidding," Kate complained, stretching up on her tiptoes. "I need a stepladder."

"Or Alex," Abby teased, referring to her older brother, who happened to be Kate's fiancé.

Grace groaned. "Just tell me when it's over."

"Five dollars...ten. Do I hear fifteen? Fifteen dollars for this lovely basket and the company of the lovely lady who prepared it. *Twenty!* Do I hear twenty-five—"

"Thirty dollars."

"Now you're talking." The mayor tucked a thumb inside his brocade vest and strutted across the stage as the crowd cheered, caught up in the friendly competition. "My wife tells me there's one slice of peach pie in here, which means you'll have to get close enough to share."

Abby nudged her. "That was smart."

"Smart had nothing to do with it," Grace muttered. "I got hungry last night."

After returning home from that unexpected encounter with Cole, it had been pie or a pint of rocky road. She'd opted for the treat with a calorie count that didn't cross over into the triple digits.

"Thirty dollars—who will give me thirty-five?" Mayor Dodd's eyes narrowed. "The money is for a good cause, gentlemen! New playground equipment for the park—"

"Fifty dollars."

A second of absolute silence followed the bid. Even Kate was rendered momentarily speechless.

"Fifty dollars. Going once—" Mayor Dodd slammed the gavel down as the crowd began to cheer. "Sold! For fifty dollars."

"That's more than Quinn paid for mine." Abby exchanged a grin with Kate.

"Come up here and get your basket." Mayor Dodd held it up like a trophy. "And your girl."

Grace wished the earth would open up and swallow her as she slowly made her way toward the stage.

She'd heard a rumor that Tom Braddock had been bragging to everyone in their department that he was going to win her basket. Tom had asked her out several times over the past few years but Grace had politely declined, using the excuse that it wasn't wise to date a coworker.

It was safer than admitting the real reason.

But Tom glared at her when she walked past, as if it was her fault that someone had outbid him.

"Don't be shy now, Grace," the mayor boomed, twirling the end of his mustache. "It's all in good fun, you know."

Grace tacked on a smile and looked around, ready to thank whoever had emptied his wallet for the new playground equipment.

And her gaze locked with Cole's. Everything else disappeared as they stared at each other.

"Hi."

"Hi." Grace's lips shaped the word, but she wasn't sure if she said it out loud.

"I hope you don't mind." Cole flashed a crooked smile. The one that had had Grace's heart spinning pirouettes when she'd been a naive teenager.

"Mind?" she repeated. Because that smile stripped her of the ability to form a complete sentence, let alone a complete thought.

Instead of answering, Cole held something up.

A basket with a bright pink bow.

"It looks like we'll be having lunch together," he said.

Lunch.

If only it were that simple, Grace thought with rising panic. But she wasn't about to tell Cole that by bidding on her basket, he hadn't simply agreed to spend an hour in her company. He was now her date for the square dance that evening and—Grace swallowed hard as another, more ter-rifying thought occurred to her—another event scheduled for the next day. One that would ruin any attempts Grace might have made to avoid Cole's company.

"What did you do?"

Watching Grace march toward him, Cole decided it had to be a trick question. Because the answer seemed pretty obvious to him.

"I bid on your basket." And he'd *won*.

But Grace squeezed her eyes shut, giving Cole the dis-tinct impression that when she opened them again, she was hoping he wouldn't be there.

Maybe she'd rather have lunch with the guy in the purple tie. Because it sure didn't look like she was thrilled with the prospect of spending time with *him*.

Regret sliced through Cole. There'd been a time when Grace had welcomed his company. When she'd welcomed his arms around her…

And there was another reason he shouldn't have taken part in the auction. Life had taken them down different roads. They'd been kids that summer. Cole was a different person now and so was Grace.

The hunted look she cast over her shoulder proved it.

"Come with me," she muttered. "We have to get out of here before…"

They were surrounded. By a group of women wearing bonnets.

Grace closed her eyes.

Maybe she was hoping *they* would disappear, too.

"I don't believe we've met." A stunning blonde with sil-ver-green eyes smiled up at him. "I'm Abby O'Halloran."

"Cole Merrick." Given the way the women were dressed,

in full skirts that skimmed the tops of their black, button-down shoes, Cole resisted the temptation to bow.

Grace sighed. "Cole, these are my...friends. Abby O'Halloran, Emma Sutton, Zoey Wilde and Jenna McGuire."

All four of the women were close to Grace's age but Cole didn't recognize their faces. He hadn't socialized much when he'd lived in Mirror Lake. Between summer school and keeping his three younger siblings entertained, there hadn't been time to hang out with the other teenagers.

Only Grace.

"Hello." Cole added a smile because they looked a lot more friendly than his former neighbor at the moment.

Four pairs of eyes blinked. In unison.

"Here." Zoey Wilde, a slim brunette with pearl-gray eyes, flipped open a cardboard fan and handed it to Grace. "I have a feeling you're going to need this more than I am."

Cole had no idea what she meant, but Grace's cheeks turned the same shade of pink as the ribbon tied around the handle of the basket.

"Yes. Well. Cole and I should be going now. Mayonnaise in the chicken salad." Grace grabbed his elbow and propelled him forward. Toward the parking lot.

They managed to make it ten steps before their escape route was blocked by a petite redhead.

"Hi, Grace. *Cole.*" Kate Nichols's shamrock-green eyes sparkled up at him. "I didn't think you were going to stick around for the celebration."

Neither had Cole.

"Marty Sullivan isn't scheduling appointments until Monday. His wife mentioned he was here, so I was hoping to track him down." Hoping to convince the lawyer to make an exception when he'd spotted Grace standing near the stage. Beautiful. Confident. *Nervous.*

Kate tipped her head and a flame-colored curl sprang free

from the bonnet. "You'll probably see Sully at the square dance tonight."

"I won't be in town that long."

"But you have to—" Kate clamped her lips together, sealing off the rest of the words.

Probably because, out of the corner of his eye, Cole saw Grace vigorously shaking her head and making a slashing motion across her throat.

He frowned. "Have to what?"

Kate looked at the sky, as if she expected to find the answer written in the clouds. "Um, tour the historical museum? There's a great...*thimble* collection. Not to be missed."

"Then we should probably make our way over there, sweetheart," a voice interjected smoothly. "Before the line gets too long."

"Alex." Kate turned to the man who'd sauntered up behind them and smiled, tucking her arm through his. "This is Cole Merrick. He used to live in Mirror Lake. Cole, my fiancé, Alex Porter."

Cole recognized the wealthy hotelier's name instantly. He just couldn't believe that Kate Nichols, who looked as sweet and wholesome as one of the apple pies in the dessert case at the Grapevine café, had ended up engaged to someone like Porter. Cole didn't know the man personally, but he knew the type. He flew them from city to city, waiting on the runway while they closed million-dollar deals over lunch. The bread and butter of Cole's charter service.

"Merrick." Alex extended his hand, his grip testing Cole's character. The jade-green eyes, his intentions.

Grace cleared her throat.

"Okay!" Kate said brightly. "Alex and I should probably leave you two alone so you can get acquainted. He has to judge the pie eating contest at two o'clock."

Cole waited for everyone to laugh at the joke. No one did.

Alex tucked Kate against his side. And then flicked a look at Cole. "Take care."

Of Grace.

Cole didn't miss the subtle warning.

At least now he understood why Grace had been in such a hurry to leave. Under different circumstances, Cole might have been offended by Porter's protective behavior. But for some reason, it was good to know Grace had people looking out for her.

"Is that everyone?" he teased as the couple strolled away.

"Not even close," Grace murmured. She hiked up the hem of her gown and started off again, dodging the other picnickers as if she was the Packers star quarterback going for a touchdown.

Cole followed at a more leisurely pace, carefully fixing his gaze on the yellow ribbons dangling from Grace's bonnet and not on the intriguing sway of her…bustle.

"How about right there?" Cole pointed to a spindly oak tree, its sparse branches creating a patch of shade not much larger than the picnic basket he was carrying.

Grace hesitated.

"Or we could always eat lunch between those two pickup trucks over there."

She nibbled on her lower lip, clearly tempted by the suggestion.

"I was kidding, Grace."

"Oh." The flash of disappointment on her face was almost comical. "I suppose the tree will be fine."

"Everything looks great." Cole lowered himself to the ground and relocated a June bug lumbering through the grass while Grace snapped open a square of gingham flannel that matched the ribbon on her basket.

"Thank you." She began to unpack the dishes and arrange them on the blanket, careful not to brush up against him.

"Beautiful day." Cole waded into the silence.

"It's supposed to be sunny and warm today and tomorrow."

"Looks like there's a pretty good turnout."

Grace nodded. "Yes."

And they were back to making small talk. But because Cole had started it with the weather comment, he couldn't really complain, now could he?

"Everyone's been talking about the celebration for months. A lot of people can trace their ancestors all the way back to the year the town was settled." Grace was using her tour guide voice now. "The planning committee spent most of the winter researching local history and we had a chance to read through some of the old letters and diaries the family members kept."

Cole glanced at the white petticoat peeping out from below the ruffled hem of her dress. "I see they kept their ancestors' clothes, too."

Except for the cowboy boots. Grace had been wearing them the night before, another small but charming glimpse of the girl he'd fallen for that summer. Before he'd been forced to put his own dreams and plan aside.

"The historical society let us borrow them for the weekend." Grace tugged off her bonnet and drops of sunlight splashed between the leaves, highlighting threads of mahogany in her hair. "It was Kate's idea. A creative way to help people remember the past."

Unfortunately, Cole wasn't having a difficult time doing that. Not with Grace sitting less than two feet away from him, carefully removing the crust from her sandwich....

"What are you looking at?"

Cole's lips quirked. "You still don't eat your crusts."

"No." Grace glanced down at her plate. "Because they still taste like crusts."

The simple logic—and the way Grace's nose wrinkled—made Cole smile. "I just figured that removing the crusts from a piece of bread was something a person…outgrew."

"Do you eat mushrooms?"

Cole couldn't prevent a shudder. "No."

"Why not?"

"Because they taste like mushrooms?"

"So in other words, a strong aversion to a particular food isn't something a person necessarily outgrows."

"It's not a strong—" Cole stopped. "I guess not."

Grace smiled.

Okay. They were having a conversation about crusts and mushrooms, but at least it was a conversation. And he'd coaxed a smile from her.

Cole considered that progress.

Until Grace chucked her half-eaten sandwich back in the basket.

"I'm sorry I don't have a lot of time, but the first tour starts in an hour and I have to get B.C. hitched up to the wagon." She rose to her feet. "Don't rush, though. Just leave the basket on the stage and I'll pick it up when you're…"

Gone? Cole was tempted to fill in the blank while Grace searched for a *polite* word.

"…finished."

He couldn't help but wonder if she would have cut the time short if Shaggy or the guy in the purple tie had placed the highest bid.

But it was probably for the best if he and Grace parted company. The same conclusion Cole had reached twelve years ago.

"There you are!"

Cole turned at the sound of a familiar voice and saw the auctioneer chugging toward them across the lawn.

"You left before I had a chance to give you this." The

man stopped at the edge of the blanket and waved an envelope under Grace's nose. "It's the roster with the names of the people who signed up for your first tour."

"Thank you, Mayor." She practically snatched it out of the man's hand.

"You look familiar." The man's attention shifted to Cole now. His snow-white mustache, waxed into points, hung from the shelf of his upper lip like icicles. "Do you have family around here?"

Cole didn't know what to say, not sure he was comfortable claiming a relationship with Sloan, one based solely on DNA.

To his surprise, Grace stepped into the silence. "This is Cole Merrick, Mayor Dodd."

"Sloan's grandson?"

"That's right." The words stuck in Cole's throat.

"Sloan would be thrilled to know you're back, son." The mayor clapped him on the back. "That piece of land meant a lot to him."

Cole smiled.

"It means a lot to me, too, sir."

The down payment on a new plane.

Chapter Four

"I wanna drink, Mama!"

Grace heard the cheerful announcement a split second before a preschool girl popped up on the other side of the beverage table set up in the corner of Daniel Redstone's barn. A pair of big blue eyes locked on the glass dispenser of ice-cold lemonade that Grace had filled before the square dance started.

"All right." The girl's mother repositioned the sleeping infant cradled in her arms and smiled at Grace. "We'll take one cup, please."

Grace ladled the lemonade into a plastic cup and the woman reached for it at the exact moment her daughter tugged on the strap of the diaper bag to get her attention. It started a chain reaction. Lemonade sloshed over the side of the cup, soaking the mother's shirt, and the baby woke up.

The woman's smile disappeared as a piercing cry rent the air.

"Here, Mama!" The girl snatched a napkin from the stack and the rest of them followed, sliding off the table like a miniature avalanche.

Now the woman looked as if she were about to burst into

tears. She tried to bend down to pick up the napkins and the diaper bag bumped a corner of the table.

"Let me help," Grace said quickly as the tower of plastic cups began to sway. She reached for the diaper bag, but suddenly found herself holding the baby, swaddled in a blue blanket, instead.

"Thank you." The children's mother began to blot the moisture from her shirt with one of the napkins as she collected the rest of them from the ground. Once Grace recovered from her initial surprise, she smiled down at the infant in her arms.

"Hey, sweetie," she whispered. "Do you have a smile for me?"

To Grace's wonder, he stopped crying immediately and stared up at her, his expression changing from absolute misery to utter delight in the blink of an eye. The scent of baby powder and lotion washed over Grace, sweeter than anything she would find at a perfume counter. The tiny legs pedaled inside the blanket and Grace chuckled.

"How many do you have?"

Grace glanced up and met the woman's knowing gaze.

"How many?" she repeated.

"Children."

"I...none."

"Really?" The look of astonishment on the woman's face was flattering. "You look like someone who knows her way around babies."

The compliment wrapped around Grace's heart like a hug.

"Not yet," she murmured, reluctantly turning the baby over to his mother.

The woman planted a kiss on her son's downy head. "Well, you will someday," she declared. "And trust me, even with all the commotion and chaos, there's nothing better than being a mom."

As Grace watched the family make their way over to one of the benches that lined the interior walls of the barn, the secret she'd been keeping stirred in her heart and brought a smile to her face.

In God's timing, when the adoption agency she'd been working with finally called, she would discover that particular truth for herself....

"Is the lemonade free?"

A pack of adolescent boys jockeyed for position in front of the beverage table and Grace smiled. "Yes, it is."

When they left five minutes later, Grace had to refill the dispenser and open another package of napkins. She was in the process of filling more cups of lemonade in anticipation of another wave of thirsty dancers when the hairs on the back of her neck stood up. The temperature rose several degrees, weighting the air and making it difficult to breathe.

Two possibilities collided and neither one would bring the evening to a pleasant conclusion.

Either she was having some kind of allergic reaction to the egg salad or...

Grace slid a cautious, sideways glance at the entrance of the barn. The ladle in her hand tipped sideways, sending a stream of lemonade running down the side of the cup and onto the checkered tablecloth.

What is going on, Lord? If this is some kind of test, I should have had a chance to study for it!

Because Cole was framed between the rough-hewn timbers of the doorway, backlit by the setting sun as if he'd been photoshopped there. A day's growth of beard shadowed his angular jaw and the strands of dark hair across his forehead were carelessly mussed. The sleeves of his lightweight cotton shirt were rolled back to reveal tanned forearms. Both hands tucked into the front pockets of faded, boot-cut jeans.

It wasn't fair that the casual look totally *worked* for him, Grace thought.

The square dance had started less than an hour ago, but if she had a dollar for every time someone had asked her about the "gorgeous guy" who'd bid on her basket, the city council wouldn't need the money they'd raised at the box social. Grace could have singlehandedly funded the new playground equipment at the park herself.

Not only that, Kate and Abby had ambushed her in the parking lot, anxious to hear all the details about the lunch she and Cole had shared.

Her friends had all become engaged or married over the past few years and for some reason, it wasn't enough that they'd found their happily ever after. They were committed to making sure that Grace found hers, too.

They weren't happy to discover that he wasn't going to be at the dance.

"I don't understand," Kate had huffed. "Jenna and Dev were standing right next to Cole during the auction and she said that he looked thrilled when he won your basket. What's the matter with him?"

Grace remained silent, knowing there probably wasn't anything wrong with Cole. But based on the way her heart started thumping like a bass drum whenever he smiled, there was definitely something wrong with *her*.

Because Grace had already been exposed to that smile, you'd think she would have built up, oh, some sort of *immunity* over the years.

During the short amount of time they'd spent together at the box social, she'd had to remind herself—frequently— that Cole wasn't her friend. He was the one who'd broken her heart.

But the most disturbing thing was, Grace couldn't quite shake the feeling that he possessed the power to do it again.

She watched Cole begin to weave his way between the clusters of people. Her gaze skipped ahead of him in a panicked attempt to guess his destination.

And landed on Kate and Abby, taking a break from the dancing on one of the wooden benches that lined the wall.

Her friends looked up as Cole stopped right in front of them.

Don't be paranoid, Grace chided herself. *Just because he hasn't left town yet, it doesn't mean he's looking for you.*

Abby and Kate were both laughing now at something that Cole said, as if they'd known him for years. Then they exchanged a knowing look that made Grace's blood run cold.

Don't do it! she silently pleaded. *Don't. Do. It.*

Two hands lifted. Two fingers pointed in her direction.

And Grace took cover behind the nearest post.

"That's strange." Abby O'Halloran rose to her feet, a frown puckering her forehead. "I just saw Grace behind the beverage table a few seconds ago."

Cole shifted his weight and tried to see over the heads of the couples that whirled past him. Given the number of people packed in the barn, the entire population of Mirror Lake must have turned out for the event.

The space behind the beverage table was empty. Where had she...

Cole saw a dab of yellow calico peeking out from behind one of the weathered support beams.

"Thanks." He smiled at Grace's friends. "I'll head over there and see if I can find her."

"I'm glad you changed your mind about escorting Grace to the dance tonight," Kate said.

Changed his mind?

If it hadn't been for Candy Sullivan, Cole wouldn't

have known that he was *supposed* to be Grace's escort that evening.

After she'd left him, Cole had finished his lunch and set out to find the elusive Marty Sullivan. The man had managed to elude him all afternoon, but Cole had received a tip—from a guy collecting aluminum cans in the alley—that Candy Sullivan always checked her bid on eBay before she locked up for the day. Cole set up a stakeout at the law office and waited. Sure enough, his informant was right. Candy had shown up sixty seconds before closing time.

"I know this is probably a bad time—" He had followed her inside and flashed what he'd hoped was a charming smile.

Candy hadn't been charmed.

"Can't whatever business you have with Marty wait until Monday morning?" She'd glared at him over her computer monitor. "Some things are more important than business, you know."

Right. Things like box socials, square dances, Pin the Tail on the Donkey and whatever else was in the works for Mirror Lake's birthday celebration.

Finally acknowledging that resistance was futile, Cole had given in. "When *will* he have time to meet with me?"

"Monday morning. Nine o'clock." Candy scooped up a snakeskin purse roughly the size and shape of a bicycle tire from the floor. "Now you better get on over to the Redstones' place before Grace thinks you stood her up."

"Stood her up?"

"You won her basket at the box social, you're her date."

"For the square dance?"

"For everything." Before Cole had a chance to ask Candy to clarify that cryptic response, she marched to the door, grumbling. "The last thing a woman needs is a guy who won't step up to the plate and do the right thing."

The words had continued to cycle through Cole's mind on his way to the parking lot.

He *had* done the right thing.

It was the reason he'd left Mirror Lake.

And Grace.

When a large, masculine hand curled around the beam a few inches above her head, Grace realized she should have hidden behind something larger. Like a bale of hay. Or the rain barrel.

She dared to look up and found herself neatly trapped in a pair of cedar-green eyes.

"Cole."

"Grace." The crooked smile made an appearance, but it wasn't the boyish one that she remembered. This was a potent, take-no-prisoners *grown-up* smile. And it packed more of a wallop than Delia Peake's cane.

She retreated to the beverage table again and poured a glass of lemonade. For herself. Because her mouth had gone as dry as the sawdust scattered on the floor.

Cole propped a hip against the side of the table, clearly in no hurry to leave. "That looks good."

"Would you like a glass?" Grace asked reluctantly, because as a member of the hospitality committee, it was her duty to be…hospitable.

"No, thanks." He planted both hands on the table and leaned forward. "But I would like to know why you didn't tell me that I was supposed to escort you to the square dance tonight."

In a town the size of Mirror Lake, she should have known someone would spill the beans.

"You told Kate you were leaving." Grace shrugged as if it didn't matter.

Cole raked a hand through his hair, disheveling it even

more. Grace resisted the urge to smooth a wayward strand back into place, which only proved the theory that those who didn't learn from history were destined to repeat it.

"I had a few things to take care of and they took longer than I thought."

Disappointment rattled through her, bumping and bruising everything in its path.

Did you really think he stuck around so he could spend more time with you?

"Don't worry about it." Grace moved the pitcher to cover the damp spot on the tablecloth. "I don't think anyone on the planning committee took into consideration that we might get bids from outsiders today."

A shadow passed through Cole's eyes, and she felt a stab of guilt. But, she reminded herself, he was the one who'd chosen to leave.

I love this town, Grace. We could build a cabin near the water...

"There you are!"

Grace inwardly braced herself as Sissy Perkins, the local Realtor, strode up to them. She'd been aware of the curious looks she and Cole had been receiving for past few minutes. She was only surprised that Wes Collins, the editor of the *Mirror Lake Register*, hadn't gotten to them first.

"Sissy, this is—"

"My newest client, according to Candy," Sissy flipped a panel of dark hair over her shoulder and aimed a megawatt, sign-on-the-dotted-line smile at Cole.

"Client?" Grace echoed.

"That's right." Sissy nodded. "Sloan Merrick's place."

"You're *selling* it?"

The words slipped out of Grace's mouth before she could stop them.

Cole hadn't explained why he'd come back to Mirror

Lake so Grace had assumed that Kate's letter had somehow prompted the visit. That he'd decided to check things out for himself before allowing people to tour the property.

But no. He'd come back to snip off his last tie with the town like an annoying thread dangling from the pocket of his shirt.

"Grace—" The husky rumble of Cole's voice reverberated through her.

She forced a smile.

"You don't owe me an explanation."

"Well, I wouldn't mind hearing one," Sissy declared. "That land has been in your family for years."

My grandfather's family, Cole wanted to say.

Sissy Perkins might be familiar with the town's history but it was clear she didn't know anything about his personal history. Sloan had never considered Cole's mother, Debra, a "true" Merrick.

Cole's parents had eloped two weeks after graduation and left Mirror Lake for good. Sloan had blamed Cole's mother for the fracture in their family, but failed to see his own pride had ultimately prevented it from healing.

"If you aren't interested, I can talk to someone else," Cole said evenly.

"I didn't say I wasn't interested." Sissy backpedaled so quickly the words practically left skid marks in the air. "How long are you going to be in town?"

"That depends," Cole hedged.

"On what?"

It was a good question. And he should have known the answer.

Cole watched Grace dab at an invisible stain on the tablecloth and wondered what she was thinking. He used to tease her that she couldn't keep a secret. Every one of her thoughts—every feeling—had been reflected in her eyes. But not anymore.

On the way to Mirror Lake, he'd spent several hours mentally preparing himself for the moment he walked through the front door of his grandfather's house. When he would relive those first few weeks following his father's death.

But nothing had prepared him to see Grace again.

Should he apologize for not saying goodbye? For not contacting her again after he'd left town?

Or would she think he was crazy for bringing it up? Or even worse, that he was arrogant enough to believe that she'd actually thought about him over the years?

"I'm meeting with my grand—*Sloan's*—attorney Monday morning at nine o'clock," he finally said, reluctant to talk business in front of Grace.

Although she, of all people, should understand why he felt no sentimental attachment to the property.

"Then stop by my office at ten." Sissy poured a glass of lemonade. "I'll try to take a drive out that way before we meet. Is the place in pretty decent shape?"

"No."

Cole and Sissy both turned toward Grace. Her eyes widened a little, as if she hadn't intended to join the conversation. But then she raised her chin, daring him to disagree.

He couldn't.

"It could use a little TLC." Cole refused to feel guilty about its run-down state. Forty-eight hours ago, he hadn't even known the house and land belonged to him.

Sissy's gaze bounced between him and Grace. "That's right. You two are neighbors." She flashed that bright smile again. "I've tried for years to convince Grace to sell. She could find a nice little place in town instead of living way out in the woods like that. It isn't exactly the most practical home. And all those rooms. It's waaay too big for a single woman. Unless—" Sissy tossed a sly glance in Grace's direction "—there's something you aren't telling us."

Cole couldn't help but notice that Grace didn't deny it. And was she...*blushing*?

"You look a little flushed, sweetie," Sissy said. "It *is* warm in here." She picked up a paper napkin and fanned herself. "Oops, I told Doug I'd be right back. I better scoot over there before Mayor Dodd draws the names for the competition tomorrow."

"Competition?"

"The 1800s' version of *Survivor.*" The Realtor smiled. "You didn't hear about that?"

"No." Cole glanced at Grace, but she wasn't looking at him. Her gaze was fixed on something over his shoulder. And every drop of color had drained from her face.

Cole's emergency response team training kicked in and he was at Grace's side in an instant. "Do you need some fresh air?"

"Yes," she whispered. "Can you get me some, please?"

"That might be kind of difficult." In spite of his concern, Cole wrestled down a smile. "Maybe we should go outside."

"Right. Outside." Grace lurched toward the door, but the wall of people shifted, effectively blocking her escape. Her frantic gaze bounced from person to person, looking for a space large enough to squeeze through.

"Excuse us." Cole took a step forward, but a teenaged girl cut them off.

"You can't leave now." She flashed a smile and the light reflected off the row of metal braces on her front teeth. "You won't be here if the mayor calls your name."

The expression on Grace's face made Cole wonder if that hadn't been her plan all along.

"Is there something else you forgot to tell me?" he murmured.

Grace nodded.

"Run."

Chapter Five

Grace tried not to groan when she saw Mayor Dodd making his way to the platform.

"If I could have everyone's attention!"

"You go ahead without me," she gasped. "I'll be out in a minute."

Cole didn't budge. "You're the one who needed some fresh air."

What Grace needed was divine intervention. Because she'd assumed Cole would be long gone by now. Blissfully unaware that when he'd bid on her basket, he had inadvertently set a whole new chain of events into motion.

Which might explain why she was feeling a bit nauseous.

"Welcome, friends." The mayor pitched his voice above the hum of conversation. "First of all, I'd like to thank Daniel and Esther Redstone for generously allowing us the use of their barn for the square dance this evening."

Enthusiastic applause followed the statement and the attractive, middle-aged couple who attended Grace's church smiled and waved to the crowd.

"Our little community has a lot of big things planned for the weekend and trust me, you won't want to miss out on a single one of them," Mayor Dodd continued. "Our first event starts bright and early tomorrow morning with a special competition that pays tribute to the brave men and women who settled Mirror Lake.

"Eight couples will face a series of challenges that will help everyone appreciate how difficult life was a hundred and twenty-five years ago but—" the mustache rustled along with his smile "—we also wanted to make it entertaining."

A knot formed in Grace's stomach, because she hadn't expected Cole to be at her side during this particular announcement.

"All the lovely ladies who took part in the social today agreed to have their names placed in this basket. From that group, we will choose eight participants." Mayor Dodd held up an old fishing creel. "Will the eight women—and their escorts—please join me on the stage when I call out your names?"

The fiddle player's bow danced across the strings as the mayor dipped his hand into the basket and retrieved a slip of paper.

"Our first contestant is...Sissy Perkins!"

The Realtor's shriek cut through the whoops and hollers that echoed through the barn. As she made her way toward the platform, Doug, the burly truck driver who'd won her basket, took her by the hand.

"Kate Nichols! Come on down."

Kate grinned and bobbed a curtsey at the crowd. Alex followed at a more leisurely pace as she bounded toward the stage.

Grace could feel her heart pounding in her ears, muffling the sound of the mayor's voice as he shouted another name.

What were the chances she would be chosen to participate? Over two dozen women had made baskets for the box social and only eight would be required to take part in the competition....

"Contestant number three—Haylie Owens." The mayor had pulled out another slip of paper.

The teenagers in the far corner of the room cheered and nudged Haylie and Rob Price, her blushing date, toward the other couples.

Grace held her breath as several more of her friends took their place in line. Abby and Quinn. Emma and Jake.

"And last, but certainly not least—" the mayor paused and Grace closed her eyes as he reached for the final slip of paper.

"Grace Eversea!"

Heads began to swivel in her direction, but Grace's feet were glued to the floor. Delia Peake bustled up, brandishing her pink-tipped walking cane like a sword.

"Go on, Gracie. They're waiting for you."

Grace stumbled forward as the crowd parted, clapping and shouting words of encouragement. Halfway to the platform, she realized she wasn't alone.

"I think you forgot something else." A familiar voice murmured in her ear.

"What?" Grace pushed the word past the lump of panic that had lodged in her throat when the mayor called her name.

"Me." Cole's low laugh wrapped around her heart and squeezed.

Why was he being such a good sport?

Because he had no idea what he was getting into.

Which was why, Grace decided, it was up to her to get him—*them*—out of it.

As quickly as possible.

"Each of the couples will be required to complete three different challenges, which I will announce right before the competition begins." Mayor Dodd smiled when a rumble of disappointment stirred the air and Grace realized the omission had been deliberate. The competition had been advertised as one of the highlights of the celebration, but a little mystery would fan the people's curiosity and guarantee a good turnout the following day.

"But—" the mayor motioned to someone across the room "—this might give you a hint as to what is in store for the couples."

Happy, the lanky mechanic who was almost as old as some of the buildings featured on Grace's historical tour, stepped out from the shadows, weighted down with tin buckets that clinked together like wind chimes as he ambled toward them.

"Inside the buckets that Happy is handing out is a coupon our couples can exchange for one item at the beginning of the competition tomorrow morning." The mayor's eyes twinkled. "*Agreeing* on that item just might be the first challenge some of them will face."

Laughter followed the statement, which Grace knew had been his intention.

She didn't dare look at Cole. A private picnic lunch under a shady tree was one thing, a competition in full view of the entire community was another.

"Andy will play one more song and then you can all go home and get a good night's sleep." Mayor Dodd grinned at the couples lined up in front of him. "You're going to need it!"

The fiddler began to play another lively jig as Happy paused in front of Grace.

Cole reached for the bucket at the same time she did, and their hands touched. Grace's heart began to flop around inside her chest like a freshly caught trout.

She could only hope the mayor would let her exchange her coupon for another partner.

* * *

Grace had vanished.

The last time Cole had seen her, she and the mayor had been deep in conversation.

He had a hunch what the topic of that particular conversation had been. It had occurred to Cole as he'd followed Grace to the front of the crowd, prodded by the elderly woman with a helmet of salt-and-pepper curls who resembled a swashbuckling gnome, that he'd messed up. Big time.

"I thought you might want to take a look at this." The mayor stepped in front of Cole as he was making his way to the door to find Grace. "We printed up some brochures so people could learn a little history of the town. It mentions Samuel Merrick, your great-great-grandpa. If it wasn't for him, this town wouldn't exist. But I suppose you're familiar with the story."

As a matter of fact, Cole wasn't. His dad hadn't talked about Mirror Lake very often, and Sloan wasn't the kind of man who'd propped his grandchildren on his knee and entertained them with stories about the family genealogy.

"Thanks." Cole folded up the brochure and stuck it in his back pocket, anxious to intercept Grace before she left.

"If you're looking for Grace, you just missed her," a young woman pointed to the side door.

Sometimes, Cole thought, being in a small town where everyone was privy to everyone else's business was a good thing.

As he jogged down the row of cars parked along the road, it occurred to Cole that he had no idea what kind of vehicle Grace drove. Other than a horse-drawn wagon.

"Grace's truck is the third one from the end," someone called. "Silver Ford."

"Thanks," Cole called back, unable to keep the smile out of his voice as he dodged an abandoned stroller.

A hundred feet away, he saw the silhouette of a woman with her back against the door of a compact pickup truck, the vehicle of choice in this area of the state. Grace's head was tipped toward the sky, eyes trained on a band of moonlight that spilled through a seam in the clouds. Her lips were moving, and Cole knew she wasn't talking to herself, she was talking to God.

Her strong faith had both mystified and challenged him when they'd first met. After his father died, Cole wasn't sure whether to blame God or ignore Him completely. Grace was the one who'd said it was okay to be honest and simply tell Him that.

Cole felt something inside him shift and break loose from its moorings. What would his life be like if he'd told Grace the truth about his family? Would she have waited for him? Or run in the opposite direction?

Not that it mattered now. He'd made the decision for them and never looked back.

Cole took another step forward, feeling very much like the intruder that he was.

"I'm sorry," he said quietly.

Grace started at the sound of his voice but didn't look at him. The gravel crunched under Cole's feet as he made his way to her side.

"It's not your fault." She sighed. "I should have told you the box social was the kickoff for the other events this weekend, but…"

She hadn't thought he'd stick around.

Cole was tempted to apologize, except he wasn't sure he was sorry things had worked out this way. A plan slowly began to take shape in his mind.

"So, what's the next step?" he asked.

"The next step?" she repeated cautiously. "I'll call Kate when I get home, and we'll figure something out."

"What's to figure out?"

Grace blinked. "If it's too late for me to drop out of the competition. Or if I need to find someone to take your place."

For some reason, neither one of those choices sat well with Cole.

"It's my fault you don't have a partner for this little competition tomorrow," he pointed out.

"The fact that you used the words 'little competition' only proves you have no idea what you're getting into," Grace said. "People have been talking about this for weeks. It's one of the highlights of the celebration."

"And you're trying to talk me out of competing tomorrow because?"

"You aren't going to be here." Grace's eyes met his. "Are you?"

That had been his original intention, but things had changed and Cole decided to go with it.

"You didn't plan on any of this," Grace went on. "I don't want you to feel obligated."

Obligated wasn't quite the word Cole would have chosen.

"I'll be your partner tomorrow."

The moon slipped behind a cloud and Cole could no longer see Grace's expression.

"What made you decide to stay?" she asked after a moment.

Cole smiled.

"You did."

The next morning, Grace took a slow lap around the living room, coffee cup in hand, and glanced at the clock for what had to be the hundredth time since the alarm had gone off.

Maybe Cole wouldn't show.

It wasn't like she hadn't given him an opportunity to back out of the competition.

After she'd given him a more compelling reason to stay.

Fragments of the conversation they'd had the night before circled through her memory.

What made you decide to stay?

You did.

Grace was still kicking herself over that one. She shouldn't have made the comment about Sloan's place needing a little TLC. But she'd been so rattled when Sissy announced that Cole planned to sell it that she hadn't been thinking clearly.

But because she'd brought it up, Cole had decided to stick around and tackle a few minor repairs after the competition. A win-win situation, he'd told her right before he'd left.

But even though Cole had claimed it was his fault if she were left without a partner for the competition, Grace wondered if he would have stayed if he hadn't scheduled two meetings for Monday morning.

To sell the land, as Sissy had so boldly pointed out, that had been in his family for over a hundred years.

As soon as the thought swept through her mind, Grace knew that she was being unfair. Cole's father had grown up in the brick house next door but moved away from Mirror Lake after he married Cole's mother. It had caused a rift in the family; Sloan blamed Debra for taking his son away and had never forgiven her.

Why would Cole feel any sentimental attachment to the property?

Or anything else, for that matter.

She set that thought firmly aside. She and Cole would be together for a few hours and then part company. Grace had tours scheduled in the afternoon, and Cole would be busy sprucing up the house he couldn't wait to put on the market.

He might have felt obligated to be her partner for the competition, but that didn't mean he had to accompany her to the bonfire and fireworks at Abby's bed-and-breakfast that evening or to the outdoor worship service that Matt, her pastor at Church of the Pines, planned to lead on Sunday morning.

On her way to the kitchen, Grace caught a glimpse of her reflection in the oval mirror and cringed. The white shirt-waist paired with a simple, ankle-length cotton skirt provided more freedom of movement than the gown she'd worn the day before, but the men definitely had an advantage over the women during the competition. The men didn't have petti-coats to deal with. Hopefully no one would notice she was wearing her cowboy boots.

"Grace?" A tap on the front door accompanied the low rumble of a masculine voice.

She froze. Maybe she could pretend—

"I know you're home. You're too cautious to leave the house with a candle burning."

Grace scowled at the votive in the windowsill, not sure whether she should be insulted or flattered by Cole's de-scription.

"Maybe I'm not cautious anymore," she muttered, petti-coats hissing as she strode to the door.

Cole chuckled.

Because he'd *heard* her.

To make matters worse, he looked…great. Hair still damp from a recent shower. A white T-shirt that stretched across his muscular chest and accentuated the broad shoulders.

If Grace were honest with herself, she knew it wasn't Cole's presence that had her emotions tied in knots. It was her *reaction* to his presence. Rapid pulse. Flushed cheeks. Weak knees. The side effects were so dangerous, the guy should come with a warning label from the surgeon general.

Cole's gaze swept over her and his smile widened. "Cute."

"The men are supposed to dress in costume, too."

"I didn't shave this morning, does that count?" He scrubbed a hand across his jaw.

It counted as one more reason to dive into the coat closet and stay there until Monday afternoon. Because the shadow of whiskers, combined with the spark of humor in Cole's eyes, only added to his masculine charm.

The trouble was, Grace didn't *want* to be charmed.

"Believe me, someone will find something for you to wear." Grace tried to come up with the most terrifying prospect.

"Suspenders. Red, like Marty Sullivan's."

"You aren't trying to scare me off, are you?"

"No." *Yes.* "I'll be out in a minute."

Instead of taking the hint, Cole wandered into the living room. "This is nice. I don't think I've ever been inside your house."

That's because he hadn't wanted to.

Grace had invited him over for dinner, but Cole had always come up with some kind of excuse not to meet her parents. After he'd left town, it had only affirmed the truth. Cole had never planned to continue their relationship. The deep connection she'd felt had been one-sided, and she'd been too naive to recognize the signs.

"I know it looks a little old-fashioned. A lot of the antiques belonged to my grandparents." Grace traced the tip of her finger across the wooden spine of the chintz sofa. "I haven't had the heart to change anything. It's…home."

Chapter Six

Home.

Cole felt a pinch of envy.

For the past twelve years, home had been the cramped, two bedroom trailer tacked onto the back of the hangar. After Cole had graduated from high school, he'd all but begged Cap, his former boss, to rent it out to him and his family.

He'd even offered a list of reasons why it was a good idea. The hangar would have round-the-clock security. He would be available evenings and weekends if Cap had an overnight stay somewhere.

What he hadn't told his boss was that he'd hoped his mom would feel better if she wasn't constantly surrounded with reminders of his father. Or that it was easier to keep an eye on his younger siblings—and feed them—if he could pop in for a few minutes between his other duties.

Cap had given in, claiming he could use the extra income, but Cole had a suspicion the retired Air Force pilot had grasped the situation. Shortly after Cole's family moved in, Cap had given him more responsibilities. Groomed him to take over the charter business when he retired.

Cole had done most of the remodeling himself in the evenings to make the transformation easier on his brothers and sister. He'd painted Bettina's room her favorite shade of cotton candy pink. Roamed the aisles of local home improvement stores until he found a wallpaper border printed with bright red fire trucks for his brothers. He'd even planted some flowers in the strip of dirt between the building and the driveway.

But no matter how hard he'd tried, there was one thing Cole hadn't been able to duplicate.

The life they'd had before their dad died.

He walked over to the stone fireplace and looked at the portraits arranged above the mantel. One was an informal photograph of Grace's entire family, including B.C., that had been taken under an apple tree in the Everseas' backyard.

His gaze lingered on a photograph of Grace, wearing a white mortarboard with a gold tassel and a knee-length satin gown.

If things had gone the way they'd planned, Cole would have graduated with Mirror Lake's senior class that day.

He'd thought about calling Grace to congratulate her, but that was the day one of his brothers had cut his foot open on a piece of glass while playing in the parking lot. He'd ended up loading all three of his siblings into the car and driving to the E.R. Three hours and ten stitches later, Cole had realized it was too late to call Grace.

In more ways than one.

Any thoughts of a future together had been officially put to rest that day. There was no way he could leave his family. Not until his mom got better and his siblings were old enough to take care of themselves.

As the days went by, and then the months, Cole had never second-guessed his decision.

Until now.

"Are these your nephews?" He shifted his attention to another photograph.

"My sister Ruth's children." Grace smiled. "Cameron is in second grade, and Hunter started kindergarten last fall." She came to stand beside him and the delicate scent of her perfume teased his senses. "I can't wait to see them next month. They call every Sunday evening to get a weekly critter update."

"Critter update?"

"Frogs. Toads. Crickets. Snakes. They want to know what I've seen and where." Grace reached out to straighten the oval frame, but Cole recognized it for what it was. An attempt to hide the tears shimmering in her eyes.

"I'd like to know where you saw the snakes, too," Cole said, just to see her smile again.

It worked.

"They're more afraid of you—"

"—than you are of them," Cole finished. "I think I've heard those words before."

"You might have heard them, but I don't think you ever *believed* them."

Grace's teasing comment should have lightened the moment. Instead, the air became heavy, weighted down by shared memories. Cole tried to blame it on simple nostalgia. The alternative, that time and space hadn't completely severed the connection that existed between them, was more than a little unsettling.

Grace hadn't given him any indication that she was prepared to take a trip down memory lane with him.

In fact, given the way she'd tried to let him off the hook for the competition, it didn't appear that she wanted to go *anywhere* with him.

"I'm surprised your family hasn't talked you into moving to Boston." Cole deliberately steered the conversation back to safer ground.

"They've tried," Grace admitted. "Mom drops a few hints

about the mild winters and how beautiful the ocean is every time we talk. Dad isn't quite as subtle. *'Grace Laurel Eversea. Massachusetts needs social workers, too.'"* She mimicked in a low growl.

Cole picked up a stuffed bear sitting in a rocking chair by the stone fireplace. "No wonder your nephews love to visit you. You even stock the place with toys."

To his astonishment, color bloomed in Grace's cheeks and she turned away.

"We should go." Her voice sounded strained. "The competition starts in half an hour."

Grace couldn't believe how close she'd come to telling Cole, of all people, something she hadn't even told her closest friends.

Six months ago, she'd filed the necessary paperwork with a private adoption agency and had recently been approved. The director had warned her it could take several years for an adoption to go through, but Grace trusted God's timing. She would wait and trust that God would bring the right child into her life at the right time.

There were so many children who needed a loving home and nurturing environment. Grace was confident she could provide both.

She'd already started redecorating her sister's old bedroom on the weekends, refinishing the hardwood floor and painting the walls a soothing shade of green.

Although Grace hadn't given in to the temptation to purchase a crib, she hadn't been able to resist picking up several of the cuddly baby blankets the Knit Our Hearts Together ministry had sold at a recent church bazaar. Grace had tucked them away on a shelf in the closet, away from curious eyes. And questions.

She avoided Cole's gaze as she grabbed the calico bonnet—not quite as offensive as the dreaded corset—from a hook near the front door.

There was something about Cole that had always tempted Grace to confide in him. Even at seventeen he'd had a way of looking at her, a way of listening, that had encouraged her to share her secrets.

A mistake Grace didn't plan to make again.

"Do you know anyone I can hire to clean Sloan's house?" Cole held the screen door open. "The outside isn't the only thing that could use a little attention."

The glint in his eye told Grace he hadn't forgotten the comment she'd made in front of Sissy about the property being neglected.

The comment that had made him decide to stay in Mirror Lake and partner with her for the competition.

"I can ask my friend Abby. She hires high school and college students to clean the cabins at the inn during the summer, so she would know who's reliable."

"That would be great. I don't have time to replace the orange shag carpeting or paint the walls, but it will be an improvement if someone can scrape the top layer of dust off everything." Cole held the screen door open for her. "Sissy Perkins will have to list it as a handyman's special."

There wasn't the least bit of hesitation or anxiety in Cole's voice when he talked about the sale. It was obvious he was at peace with the decision.

So why did the knot in her stomach tighten as she slipped into the passenger seat of his car?

"Grace?" His voice intruded softly on Grace's thoughts.

She turned away from the window, which brought her closer to him. So close that she could see a small, crescent-shaped scar in the cleft of Cole's chin. One that hadn't been there before.

It should have reminded her again how many years separated the present from the past. How many experiences they hadn't shared. How she shouldn't be looking forward to the one ahead.

"What exactly are we doing?"

"I have no idea." Grace sighed. A split second before she realized that Cole was referring to the competition. "The mayor insisted on keeping the details a secret until we're ready to start," she added hastily.

"I thought you were on the planning committee."

"I am, but this particular event is the mayor's baby, and he handpicked a group of people to organize it. The volunteers who participated in the box social were kept out of the loop in case our names were drawn."

"Why the big secret? It isn't like the competitors would practice the challenges if they knew what they were ahead of time…" Cole stopped when she shot him a look. "No way."

Dreams of a peaceful ride to clear her thoughts dissolved under the impact of his smile.

"If you were here at Christmas, you would know how competitive people can be," Grace said. "The mayor had to pass a special ordinance a few years ago, limiting the number of lights people could display in their yards. He claimed Mirror Lake was going to singlehandedly drain the power grid if he didn't do something."

"But you must have heard rumors. No one can keep a secret in a small town."

"I only know what he told us at the dance last night. We'll be required to complete several ordinary tasks in a certain amount of time."

"Ordinary tasks," Cole mused. "That doesn't sound too difficult."

"I should have said ordinary for 1887," Grace muttered. "I watched Eddie Gunderson unload some of his chickens into a pen behind city hall when B.C. and I had our first tour yesterday."

"Chickens?" Cole repeated, his smile growing wider. "That doesn't sound too disturbing."

Grace swallowed hard and turned her attention back to the passing scenery.

It was her heart's traitorous response to Cole's presence that Grace found disturbing.

Cole released a slow breath.

Maybe spending the morning with Grace wasn't going to be as easy as he'd thought it would be.

After he'd returned to his grandfather's house the night before, he'd called Iola to break the news that he wouldn't be returning to work until Monday afternoon. Even though his secretary was constantly after him to take a few days off, the reality was it was difficult with a business as small as Painted Skies. Every minute Cole spent offsite put an additional burden on his dedicated but already overworked crew.

Not only would Virgil have to fill in for the lessons they'd scheduled on Monday morning, but Cole also had a mountain of application forms to sign before he met with the bank on Tuesday.

But Iola had laughed when he'd said he planned to stay in Mirror Lake through the weekend. Not exactly the response he'd been expecting. She'd gone on to explain that both his students had canceled their lessons and rescheduled them for later in the week.

Then she'd tacked on a comment about God's timing being perfect.

Cole hadn't been able to argue with that. If Iola hadn't found Kate's letter when she did, he might have never found out about the inheritance. It could have taken months, if not years, to put his business expansion plan into motion.

And he wouldn't have run into Grace by the lake the evening he'd arrived.

Something, of course, he didn't dare mention to Iola. As often as the woman scolded him about not taking any time off, she scolded him more about the fact that he didn't have a "social life," which, in Iola-speak, meant a steady girlfriend.

So, to maintain the peace—*his* peace—all Cole had said was that he needed to fix a few things around his grandfather's house before he met with the Realtor Monday morning.

"Don't you dare feel guilty about spending an extra day or two," Iola had clucked. "You'll still be working toward your dream."

That's right. His dream.

Just in case he forgot the reason he'd returned to Mirror Lake.

It still didn't stop Cole from sliding a sideways look at Grace. Or tracing the lines of her profile with his eyes. The fringe of sable-brown lashes. The straight little nose. Before he was tempted to linger on the full curve of her bottom lip, Cole wrenched his gaze back on the road where it belonged.

Focus on what's straight ahead.

He had the feeling it was going to become his mantra over the next few hours. The only reason he'd come back to Mirror Lake was that God had provided an open door. One that would bring him that much closer to fulfilling his dream.

That was the important thing now, not trying to sift through his emotions regarding a certain brown-eyed girl from his past.

Chapter Seven

"Turn left by the library."

Grace pointed out the passenger-side window as Cole turned onto Main Street. "We'll probably have to walk a little ways. It's going to be hard to find a place to park."

She was right. Even though it was six-thirty in the morning, he had to drive around the block three times before he found an empty space.

Cole turned the key in the ignition and hopped out of the car. Dew still beaded the grass, but the cloudless sky was the shade of blue that promised a perfect summer day.

Above his head, a tiny glint of silver cut a path through the sky, the jet stream leaving behind a cryptic message in flowing white cursive that only another pilot could appreciate and understand.

On a morning like this, he usually couldn't wait to climb into the cockpit. Alone. Aim straight toward the clouds and watch everything below him shrink in size. Houses. Cars.

His problems.

Flying was his escape. And in a strange paradox, it was the one thing, other than his faith, that had kept him grounded over the years.

Suddenly, Cole realized that a day like this would only be perfect if Grace were at his side.

"Miss Grace!"

Cole saw a blur as two small children hurtled toward them across the lawn.

Grace immediately dropped to the ground and gathered the boy and girl into her arms. "Are you having fun?"

The younger one, a pixie with wispy blond hair and enormous periwinkle blue eyes, nodded. "Aunt Jenna says we can have ice cream after we watch the fireworks tonight."

Fireworks?

He glanced at Grace but she avoided his eyes.

"Ice cream sounds like a great idea." Rising to her feet, Grace settled the little girl on one slim hip.

"Who are you?" The boy attached himself to Grace's arm and stared up at Cole suspiciously.

"I'm Cole. Grace's teammate." He put out his hand and it was taken in a surprisingly firm grip.

"I'm Logan J. Gardner and this is my sister, Tori."

Cole tamped down a smile. "It's nice to meet you."

"Aunt Jenna said she and Dev are going to win the contest today," Logan informed them. "'Cuz Dev knows how to do all kinds of cool stuff."

"He's a wildlife photographer," Grace explained, "with survival skills."

"He can start a fire without matches, and he doesn't burn the marshmallows," Tori announced.

Grace laughed and planted a kiss on the girl's plump cheek. "I'm not sure how we can compete with that."

"Let's go, Tori." Logan grabbed his sister by the hand. "Maybe Aunt Jenna will let us play on the swings for a while."

"Cute kids," Cole said as they scampered back to a couple standing underneath the branches of one of the oak trees that dotted the park. He recognized the striking, blue-eyed blonde as Jenna McGuire, one of the four women Grace had introduced him to after the box social. The dark-haired man standing next to her had the bronzed, rugged look of someone used to spending time outdoors. "Have you known them a long time?"

Grace hesitated. "I was assigned to the Gardner family last summer, and I met Jenna when she moved to Mirror Lake to take care of the children. She's their aunt, but she was granted full custody of Logan and Tori because their mother was no longer in a position to care for them. They're doing great…"

Now.

Cole heard the unspoken word and read between the lines. There'd been a time when that hadn't been true. Grace might have been Logan and Tori's caseworker, but the affection he'd seen in her eyes, the way she'd wrapped her arms around them, said what she hadn't. The children were more than names in a file.

"Your job must be difficult," he said slowly, trying to reconcile the shy teenager with the woman who deliberately positioned herself in the middle of difficult family situations.

"It can be, but that just comes with the territory." Grace's smile, the gleam of passion in her eyes revealed her heart. It was worth it.

Maybe she'd put her plans to have a family of her own on hold because she was as dedicated to her career as he was. Something they had in common…

Whoa.

Cole put the brakes on that thought.

All he and Grace had in common was this crazy competition. They were Couple Number Eight, not a…couple.

No matter what Iola had said about God's timing.

The truth was, after trying, sometimes unsuccessfully,

to keep his twin brothers on the straight and narrow over the years and trying to keep up with the rampant drama in Bettina's life, Cole was in no hurry to repeat the process.

Not for a long time anyway.

"Five minutes!" The mayor's familiar bellow echoed through the park.

"That's our cue!" Kate dashed past, towing Alex Porter by the hand. "See you two at the starting line," she called over her shoulder. "And don't forget the bucket they handed out last night at the square dance!"

Cole glanced at Grace. "I don't remember seeing the bucket."

Grace closed her eyes.

"That's because it's still in the backseat. Of *my* truck."

How could she have forgotten the bucket?

Grace placed the blame right where it belonged. On a handsome distraction named Cole Merrick.

Lord, help me get through the next few hours without losing my mind.

Although at the moment, Grace couldn't shake the feeling there was something else she should be worried about losing.

Her heart.

The thought left her reeling.

She sensed a subtle change in Cole that she couldn't quite put her finger on. Even before his father's death, from some of the things Cole had told her, Grace got the impression he'd been what her parents referred to as a "restless soul." He had admitted that he struggled in school and ran with kids whose favorite extracurricular activity was breaking the rules.

Cole's rebellion was part of the crushing guilt that had weighed him down. He felt sure he'd disappointed his dad and the fact that he'd never had an opportunity to apologize had only added another layer to his grief.

The first time they'd met, Cole had been all sarcasm and sharp edges. The strained relationship with his grandfather hadn't done anything to improve his attitude.

As Cole had let his guard down, Grace had caught a glimpse of his heart that hinted at the man he could become if he put aside his guilt and anger.

Looking at the brief interactions they'd recently had, Grace could see that he had become that man.

It was a bittersweet feeling. Knowing she'd been right about him all along…but she hadn't been there to witness the transformation.

Hadn't she learned anything from the past?

Even though Cole had changed, he was going to walk out of her life and not look back, the way he had all those years ago.

"Come on, then. It looks like we'll have to improvise."

Cole jogged around the back of the vehicle and popped open the hatch. "Let's see what we've got in here."

Grace's mouth dropped open as he began to sort through the jumbled contents.

Two collapsible canvas chairs. A baseball bat and glove. Fishing pole. A beach towel—*pink*—with a bikini-clad penguin on the front.

"This is a landfill on wheels," Cole muttered. "My next vehicle is going to be a convertible. Hold this, please." He deposited a grass-stained soccer ball into Grace's hands.

She stared down at it, suddenly weak in the knees.

Did Cole have *children*? He wasn't wearing a wedding ring, but not all men did. It was possible he was divorced.

Once again, the realization they were little more than strangers sliced through her. Time hadn't stood still, no matter how her heart reacted when Cole cast a smile in her direction.

"This will have to work." He moved a cooler and pulled

something out from underneath a bright red-and-white Badgers stadium blanket.

Grace blinked. "Is that a *minnow* trap?"

"Right now, it's something that will hold water." Cole's lips curved. "Hopefully water we won't have to drink."

Grace tried to scrape up a smile in return as she spotted a pair of lime-green flip-flops stuffed in the corner of the trunk.

Not exactly Cole's color.

"You have…a family?"

"Of course I do." He sounded surprised by the question. "Two brothers and a sister. You've met them."

For some reason that Grace didn't want to analyze too closely, relief washed through her. Followed by confusion.

Grace did a silent calculation. The twins, Travis and Sean, would be eighteen by now. Bettina a year older. Cole was nine years older than his siblings. He would have moved out years ago. So why did he have all their paraphernalia in his vehicle?

Cole's seven-year-old sister and six-year-old twin brothers had tagged after them occasionally that long-ago summer, but Grace couldn't remember much about them. Cole had once confided that his mother had suffered several miscarriages in the years that separated him and his sister and brothers. It was one of many secrets he'd entrusted her with over the course of the summer.

Which made his abrupt departure a few weeks later even more difficult to understand.

Don't go there, Grace silently chided herself.

Nothing in Cole's behavior hinted that he'd given her more than a passing thought over the years. Or that he was interested in anything more than making up for the muddle he'd unwittingly created when he bid on her basket.

"I've been looking for this for months." Shaking his head,

Cole draped a lightweight nylon jacket over the soccer ball cradled in Grace's arms. "Bettina must have borrowed it. She's notorious for rearranging things. Furniture. Important files. She took my secretary's place for a week and somehow managed to turn the office upside down. Iola found Kate's letter a few days ago. Bettina had filed it under the letter *Q*."

"Q—" Grace smiled as understanding dawned. "Because one hundred and twenty-five years is a quasquicentennial."

"Right." Affection, not frustration, flowed below the word.

Grace took a moment to absorb the ramifications of what she'd just learned. She wasn't sure what surprised her more. Discovering that Bettina—the precocious little girl with freckles and Pippy Longstocking braids—had taken over for Cole's secretary.

Or that Cole *had* a secretary.

Grace found she could no longer contain her curiosity.

"What do you do for a living?"

"I run a private air charter service near Madison."

Grace forgot she'd made a vow to play it cool. Forgot she was determined to pretend they'd never been anything more than friends. She reached out and squeezed his hand.

"You're a *pilot*. Cole…I knew you could do it."

His fingers instantly closed around hers, forming a warm cage she realized she had no desire to escape.

"When did you get your license?" Grace swallowed hard and pretended she didn't feel the sparks of electricity that shot down her arm.

"When I was twenty." Cole's lips tipped in a wry smile. "Painted Skies is a small operation, but it looks like I'll be able to expand the business this year."

Grace heard a rushing sound in her ears as another memory crashed over her.

They were sitting on the rock, side by side, watching the clouds drift by.

That's what I want to do someday, Cole had told her. *I want to fly planes.*

So do it.

Even without closing her eyes, Grace could see the expression on Cole's face, hope and doubt battling for control.

You make it sound so easy.

Maybe you're making it too difficult, Grace had countered. *I happen to think you can accomplish anything you set your mind to.*

Cole had searched her face, and Grace hadn't wanted to look away that time because she wanted him to see the truth in her eyes. But that wasn't all he must have seen. Because he'd smiled and pulled her into his arms. And whispered that he loved her....

With a start, Grace realized Cole was still holding her hand.

And they were starting to attract attention.

Cole watched the sparkle fade from Grace's eyes as she tugged her hand free. Her expression smoothed over like the lake on a windless summer evening.

"I'm glad your dreams came true," she said quietly.

Not all of them.

The thought sprang into Cole's mind. At one time, being with Grace had been part of those dreams.

What would Grace say if he told her that *she'd* been his inspiration for pursuing his goal of becoming a pilot? Even before his father's death, he'd been flying blind, without a clear destination in mind.

Grace was the one who'd challenged him to think about the future. Encouraged him to turn what most people would have considered an impossible dream into a reality.

He'd never had the opportunity to tell her how much it had meant to him, though.

"Grace—"

"Okay, everyone! Gather around!" Mayor Dodd interrupted, his voice carrying across the park without the aid of a microphone. "I'm sure you're all anxious to get started."

The women whose names had been called the night before, along with their escorts, broke away from the group of spectators and formed a line in front of the mayor. Cole thought he heard Grace sigh as she stepped forward to join them. The couples shifted to make room and he and Grace were sandwiched between Kate and Alex Porter and Esther and Daniel Redstone, the couple who'd offered their barn for the square dance.

Mayor Dodd hooked his thumbs in his suspenders and paced down the row, his narrowed gaze sweeping over the competitors with the same intensity a military commander would eye a group of new recruits.

"My lovely wife, Rhoda, will be walking by in a few moments with a basket to collect all the little gizmos and gadgets you *won't* be needing today. None of the early settlers had iPods, iPads or iPhones. During the course of our competition, couples are not allowed to possess—or use— anything that didn't exist in 1887."

"What about sunscreen?" Sissy Perkins protested.

"Seriously?" Cole whispered. "The hat she's wearing is as big as an umbrella. She could shade a family of four underneath it."

A smile moved through Grace's eyes so swiftly that Cole thought he must have imagined it.

"Pay attention," she admonished.

Rhoda moved from couple to couple. By the time she stood in front of them, the basket was weighted down with cell phones, cameras and an assortment of personal possessions that included tissues, a plastic container of breath mints, a miniature flashlight and a calculator.

Cole had locked his wallet in the glove box of the car but peeled off his waterproof Timex and added it to the spoils. Grace dropped her cell phone and a small tube of lip balm into the basket.

"Aren't you forgetting something?" Cole raised an eyebrow.

Grace gave him a wide-eyed, innocent look. "No?"

He might have believed her if the word hadn't come out like a question. Rhoda must have thought so, too, because she paused and looked over her shoulder.

"Gracie, was there something else?"

She frowned. At him.

"It's only a few hours," Cole murmured. "Hand 'em over."

Grace opened her mouth to argue. And then closed it again, proving his hunch was correct. She still carried her favorite candy everywhere.

"Fine." She fished around in the pocket of her skirt and deposited a brightly colored package into the basket. "Here you go."

"Thank you, dear."

"Doesn't that feel better?" Cole whispered as the mayor's wife moved on to Kate and Alex. "Your pockets are lighter and so is your conscience."

"Our stomachs will be lighter, too," Grace muttered. "Especially if we're forced to rely on our hunting-and-gathering skills."

"Keeping the Skittles would have broken the 1887 rule." Cole smiled. "You could have gotten us disqualified."

Chapter Eight

Disqualified, Grace mused.

Now, why hadn't *she* thought of that?

"Don't worry," Cole said. "If you get hungry, I have an apple in my car."

Grace pulled in a breath when he winked at her, not the least bit repentant he'd made her turn over the contraband candy.

A part of her wished she could simply focus on the present and enjoy the company of an attractive man instead of getting tangled up in memories.

Maybe she should pretend they'd just met. Start fresh. Leave the past behind, the way Cole obviously had...

"Hey, you," Kate whispered. "Are you paying attention?"

"Yes."

Her friend shot a teasing glance at the man standing next to her. "I can see that." Kate lowered her voice. "But are you paying attention to the *mayor*?"

Some comments, Grace decided, didn't deserve a response.

"The section of woods by the shoreline has been divided into eight campsites, one for each couple," Mayor Dodd was saying. "You will locate the flag marked with the number in which your names were chosen last night. You will be free to move around the park, but the majority of the tasks will be completed in your designated area so that our spectators will be able to watch your progress."

"Or our humiliation," someone farther down the row mumbled.

"Now—" The spark of mischief in the mayor's eyes made Grace uneasy. He did have a flair for the dramatic. "Is everyone ready to find out what our brave men and women will be facing?"

The enthusiastic response from the crowd that had gathered to watch the competition sent a flock of mourning doves swirling into the air.

Grace watched them go, a little envious that they were able to escape.

"The first challenge will be building a campfire." The mayor grinned. "When you have successfully completed that task, return to the general store—" laughter rippled through the crowd when Mayor Dodd pointed to a popup camper parked underneath the trees a hundred yards away "—where Faye McAllister, one of our dedicated volunteers, will be waiting with an envelope. Inside that envelope is a piece of paper that will tell you what you and your partner will be making for breakfast—over the campfire you started."

"That—" Cole leaned closer and his breath stirred the hair near her ear, sending a shiver dancing up her spine "—might explain the chickens."

Grace clapped a hand over her mouth to seal off an unexpected—and totally inappropriate—burst of laughter. "This is a family-friendly event."

"Yeah?" Cole winked at her. "Tell that to the chickens."

Grace forced herself to look away.

Every one of his smiles, every comment laced with that warm, albeit slightly irreverent, humor wore away the walls she tried to keep in place. Grace had made up her mind she could survive the morning, but she hadn't considered the fact she would *enjoy* Cole's company.

"When is the next election?" Grace heard Alex mutter to Kate. "I'll find someone to run against him."

Cole slid a look at the couple. "We could always vote him off the island," he suggested.

Grace couldn't believe Cole wasn't intimidated by Alex Porter like ninety-nine percent of the general population.

"Wrong competition, unfortunately." Alex's eyes narrowed. "But I appreciate the way you think."

Cole inclined his head.

The two men didn't exactly *smile* at each other, but somehow, Grace got the impression they'd just bonded.

Kate looked at Cole and then at Grace. "I like him," she announced.

Grace didn't return the smile. She didn't want her friends to like Cole.

She didn't want to like Cole.

But the familiar tug on her heart when he looked at her, those sparks of electricity that made every nerve ending in her body hum whenever Cole was close by, made Grace wonder if it wasn't happening already.

"A-*hem*." Mayor Dodd gave them a silence-in-the-ranks frown. "Time is of the essence. When you complete one task, you will immediately go on to the next one. The first couple to complete all of the challenges in two hours will win the grand prize."

Cole nudged her elbow. "You never said anything about a grand prize."

That was because it happened to be dinner for two at Abby's bed-and-breakfast. Alex had generously offered the services of his head chef from Porter Lakeside in Chicago for the event.

The thought of sharing a romantic evening with Cole conjured up equal amounts of hope and terror.

"When the whistle blows, head over to the general store. You may trade your coupon for the item you feel will help you the most during the competition."

Oh. *No.*

"Cole." His name came out in a squeak. "The coupon…"

"Is in the bucket," he guessed. "In the backseat of your car."

Grace could only nod.

"No problem." One broad shoulder lifted and fell. "It will make things more interesting."

"I like him, too," Abby said, not bothering to hide the fact she'd been eavesdropping.

Grace hadn't noticed her other friend had managed to sidle closer to her and Cole. Abby and Kate were a force to be reckoned with when they focused on a common goal.

A terrifying possibility suddenly occurred to Grace. Getting her and Cole together might be that common goal. As soon as she had a chance to speak to her friends, she'd set them straight.

"Your third and final task—" the mayor paused dramatically and everyone leaned into the silence, anxious to hear what he was going to say "—will be building a temporary shelter."

Please, God, very temporary, Grace thought, because she'd come up with a plan of her own in the last sixty seconds. To put as much space between her and Cole as possible. It was the only way she was going to make it through the morning.

"A couple of branches." Rob Price grinned at Haylie. "That'll be easy."

The mayor heard him.

"The shelter has to be large enough for two and able to protect its occupants from the elements," he announced. "And wild animals."

"Should we be concerned about the chipmunks?" Cole frowned. "Because I thought they looked kind of friendly."

Grace pressed her lips together to seal off a smile.

The mayor paused and nodded at Happy, who put two fingers in his lips and let out a piercing whistle.

No one moved.

Mayor Dodd leaned forward and propped his hands on his knees as he surveyed the couples lined up in front of him.

"That means *go.*"

Cole grabbed Grace's hand.

"Because we don't have a coupon, we're going need something to barter," he said as they started toward the general store.

"Barter?"

"It was a common practice back then, so technically we won't be breaking any rules."

"My bonnet?"

Cole smiled at the hopeful note in Grace's voice but shook his head. "No way. You'll get sunburned."

"What about this?" Grace touched the elastic band around her ponytail.

"Only if the owner of the general store is in a good mood."

"I wouldn't count on it. Faye McAllister doesn't exactly have a reputation for her easygoing personality."

"Maybe she won't ask for the coupon."

"It's Faye McAllister," Grace repeated. "She'll ask. You should have let me keep the Skittles."

Cole glanced down at her, saw the teasing light in her eyes, and the temperature in the air shot up another ten degrees.

"So, we have to make a fire, something to eat and build a shelter, but we're allowed to choose only one item from the general store. What do you think?"

"I think the mayor just lost the next election," Grace muttered.

"Hey, you two!" Emma Sutton sang out as she and her husband loped past. "The clock is ticking."

That's when Cole realized he and Grace had stopped in the middle of the park. And he was still holding her hand.

Grace stumbled away from him and they followed the couples making their way toward the camper. Jenna and Dev McGuire were already at the front of the line, with Esther and Daniel Redstone right behind them.

A woman with rooster-red hair handed Daniel a hatchet and then turned to Cole.

"Coupon," she barked.

Grace eased in front of Cole. "I'm sorry, Faye. I left it at home," she confessed.

The woman's eyebrows began to slide together over her nose.

"But we can barter for an item, right?" Cole wasn't going to let Grace take all the blame.

The older woman's gaze shifted to him and Cole found himself being examined like a bug under a microscope.

"Merrick," she declared.

"That's right."

"I knew it." Faye shook her head. "You've got your grandpa's stubborn chin."

Cole didn't know what to say. He'd assumed Faye had heard about his arrival. He and his grandfather shared the same last name, but he'd never considered the fact there was a family resemblance.

Probably because Sloan had never treated him as a member of the family.

Grace saw surprise—and some darker emotion—flared briefly in Cole's eyes. The same expression Grace had seen there when Happy had recognized him at the square dance.

Cole didn't seem to understand it didn't matter that he'd

never lived in Mirror Lake more than a few months. In people's minds, his family had put down roots in the area a long time ago. No matter how Cole felt about Sloan or the town, he was a branch on the Merrick family tree.

"Does that mean we can trade?" Cole tipped his head. And unleashed the full power of his smile.

Grace didn't have a chance to tell him that he was wasting his time. Faye wouldn't fall for such blatant charm...

Or maybe she would.

Grace watched in astonishment as the woman...melted. One blue-veined hand fluttered—*fluttered*—to the spot just above her heart.

"And you've got your daddy's smile," Faye acknowledged wryly. "All right, what have you got?"

Cole shot Grace a questioning look. "What have we got?"

"I'm not sure." Grace's fingers crept to the collar of the white shirtwaist she wore and touched the gold charm below the fabric, a nervous habit left over from the days when she'd barely been able to look people in the eye.

Faye noticed.

"A necklace?" she harrumphed. "I suppose that will do."

The air emptied out of Grace's lungs. "I don't—"

"That's a great idea." Cole looked so relieved that Grace didn't have the heart to refuse. And it wasn't as if they had another option.

"Don't worry." Faye held out her hand. "I'll take good care of it."

Grace's heart began to pound as she carefully tried to extract the delicate chain until the tiny gold bird on the end of the chain was free.

Her fingers fumbled with the tiny clasp, which of course, because of the way things had been going the past twenty-four hours, ended up getting tangled in a strand of her hair.

"Let me help."

Before she could protest, Cole's hands brushed hers aside. The warmth of his touch sent tingles down her spine. For a moment, she felt him go still.

Did he recognize it?

Grace held her breath as Cole draped the delicate gold chain over his palm and presented it to Faye.

His expression didn't change.

It was obvious Cole didn't remember the necklace.

Or the promise he'd made when he'd given it to her.

Chapter Nine

Don't read too much into it, Cole told himself.

The fact that Grace happened to be wearing a necklace he'd given to her as a gift didn't mean she'd been pining away for him for twelve years.

It probably didn't mean anything at all.

Faye McAllister cleared her throat and made a point of snapping open an ornate pocket watch. A not-so-subtle hint that he and Grace were holding up the line.

Cole scanned the eclectic collection of merchandise displayed on low wooden benches. Several cast iron skillets. A blue enamel coffeepot. A spool of twine.

The campfire would be the key to their success, especially given the fact the second challenge was making something to eat.

"We'll take a flint if you have one."

"Dev and Jenna already took it," Faye informed him. "There aren't any duplicates. The first couple gets first pick of the merchandise."

"The mayor didn't mention that," Grace protested.

"The mayor didn't mention I'm judging the cooking part of the competition, either." Faye looked smug. "But I am.

You have ten seconds and then, in the interest of time, I'm going to pick something for you."

"What about that canvas tarp?" Grace pressed closer, and the scent of something light and sweet stirred the air.

Lilacs.

Cole was beginning to realize that even the smallest, most insignificant, things had the power to trigger a memory.

The way Grace fiddled with her necklace when she was nervous. Blushed when people teased her.

Read his mind.

He smiled. "You always knew what I was thinking, didn't you?"

Instead of answering, Grace pivoted away in a swirl of white petticoats. "I'm going to start looking for kindling," she called over her shoulder.

Cole was about to remind her that would violate the rule about working together as a team, but Faye rapped him on the back of his hand with a wooden spoon.

"Do you want my advice?"

He had a hunch there was only one correct answer to that question.

"Sure."

"Keep your eye on the prize and don't mess this up." Faye plucked the tarp from the shelf and handed it to him.

"We'll do our best to win."

Faye's eyes rolled toward the sky. "I wasn't talking about the competition, honey."

Cole was mulling over the woman's cryptic words when he caught up to Grace a few seconds later. She was making her way toward the old-fashioned pump, the handle of the minnow bucket looped over her arm like a designer purse.

"McGuire might be a wildlife photographer, but I'm guessing those two are going to be the toughest ones to beat." Cole nodded at Daniel and Esther Redstone. "They have age and experience on their side."

Grace looked at him now, eyes wide with disbelief. "You're actually enjoying this, aren't you?"

"Aren't you?" Cole tossed back.

Grace didn't answer, which was, he decided, an answer in itself.

Was it the competition she wasn't looking forward to? Or spending time in his company?

If Cole were honest with himself, he had to admit he was looking forward to the next few hours.

He also had to admit the spark of attraction was still there. It was tempting to blame the sudden, unexpected spikes in his heart rate on the heat. Or simple nostalgia. A reasonable response to being reunited—even temporarily—with the first girl he'd ever fallen for.

But Grace, the pretty but shy girl next door, had grown into a beautiful, confident woman.

A beautiful woman who was even more intriguing than the challenges the mayor had given them to complete.

"Should we fill our bucket first or find the flag?"

"The bucket," Grace said. "But I'm *not* drinking from it."

Cole shook his head. "Where is that can-do, pioneer spirit that's going to help us win this competition?"

"I think it's with our coupon."

There it was again. That *almost*-smile.

Cole added another challenge to the list the mayor had given them.

Get Grace to laugh. Out loud.

"Cole Merrick!"

Sissy Perkins and Doug, wearing faded dungarees over a collarless shirt, were already in line at the pump when they got there.

The Realtor's eyes lit up and she grabbed both his hands

as if they'd known each other for years. "I thought you'd find a way to get out of this. Aren't you supposed to be fixing up some things on that old place so we can get it on the market faster?"

Yes, he was. But strangely enough, Cole hadn't thought of his to-do list for quite a while.

Right about the time he'd seen Grace standing at the front door.

"This is important, too."

"You're a smart man!" Sissy finally released him. "All these potential buyers in one place. I'm glad you're taking advantage of the situation."

Grace refused to look at Cole as he filled the bucket with water.

She hadn't considered the possibility that no matter what Cole had claimed, he'd had an ulterior motive for agreeing to take part in the competition. But Sissy had raised a valid point. Ninety percent of the local population had gathered for Mirror Lake's birthday party. It would be the perfect time to let everyone know his plans. Even in a struggling economy, property with lake frontage was always a sound investment. It wouldn't be unrealistic to predict Cole would have interested buyers lining up to take a look at the property.

What was unrealistic was Cole changing his mind about selling.

And why would you want him to? an inner voice chided.

He lied to you.

He *left* you.

It wasn't the kind of foundation that would encourage her to trust him again.

If only her heart was in line with what her head knew to be true....

"Grace?" Cole had filled the bucket and was striding away from the pump. "Ready to find our flag?"

She was ready to forfeit, that's what she was ready to do. But then she'd have to explain—to her friends and the mayor and all the people watching—*why* she wanted to forfeit. Which left her with no choice but to follow Cole.

They worked their way through the maze of lawn chairs and blankets the spectators used to stake their claim to watch the fun.

Abby smiled and gave Grace a thumbs-up behind Cole's back as they passed the O'Hallorans bright yellow flag.

Grace gave her friend a warning look that only pushed Abby's smile into a full-blown grin.

"There it is." Cole pointed to a green flag emblazoned with the number eight. "Home sweet home."

Grace's gaze swept over their designated area. The small campsite was only steps away from a natural curve in the shoreline, bordered with golden sand and patches of wild blue and pink forget-me-nots. Cattails swayed in time to the soft lap of the waves and the breeze that danced over the water.

Even though their designated area was only ten yards away and a small crowd had turned their lawn chairs toward the campsites to watch the competition, Grace was suddenly aware that for the next few hours, it would be just the two of them. Working side by side. Together.

Cole weighted down the tarp with a rock, brushed the dust from his hands and turned to look at her. "Well, come on, woman. We need a plan. And a fire."

Grace parked her hands on her hips. "Did you just call me *woman?*"

The young couple that had spread a blanket on the ground several yards away snickered.

Cole shrugged. "I'm not wearing a costume. I have to do what I can to make things seem more authentic."

"Except you're supposed to be a lumberjack, not Cro-Magnon man."

"Sorry." Cole laughed and the sound went straight through her defenses and wrapped around her heart. Twice.

Focus, Grace.

She folded her arms across her chest. "Do you happen to have any idea how we're going to start a fire?"

"You didn't happen to bring a book along, did you?"

Grace had a flashback of the day they'd met and decided the only way she was going to make it through the competition was to pretend she didn't know what Cole was talking about.

Pretend she hadn't once been head over heels, hopelessly in love with him.

But that was a challenge Grace suddenly had her doubts she would win.

Cole watched Grace fiddle with the collar of her pristine white shirt.

Was he making her nervous?

Or simply uncomfortable?

Neither one had been his intention.

In some ways, the summer they'd met seemed like a lifetime ago, but it remained as clear in his memory as if it had taken place yesterday.

Cole wasn't sure why it was so important that Grace acknowledge she remembered the time they'd spent together, too. Maybe because getting to know her had impacted him on so many levels. She'd corrected his homework. Shared her faith. Listened to him vent his frustration about his grandfather. Helped him through those difficult weeks following his father's death.

Because Grace had given so much to him, he'd decided

to return the favor the only way he knew how. By leaving her alone.

Cole convinced himself she would get caught up in the busyness of her senior year and forget about him.

Now that it seemed as if his theory had proven correct, the disappointment that surfaced didn't make sense.

Unless you want to pick up where you left off.

He yanked the thought back in line. Better to take his cue from Grace and stick to a challenge that wouldn't be as difficult.

Like starting a fire without matches.

It was sure a lot safer than thinking about rekindling a former romance.

And speaking of rekindling…Cole's nose began to twitch.

He spun around and saw their closest competitors kneeling beside their circle of stones, feeding tiny sticks to the fire merrily glowing in the center.

A cheer went up from the crowd of teenagers nearby.

"I don't believe it," Cole muttered.

The girl, a willowy blonde with bright blue eyes, heard him and a wide smile broke out across her face. "Look, Grace!"

"You two have a good start, Haylie," she called.

The teenager bobbed her head. "Dev and Jenna got their fire going right away, so Rob and I told them we would give them our cast iron skillet in exchange for letting us borrow their flint for ten minutes. We got the idea when we saw you give Faye your necklace."

"Is there a penalty for stealing trade secrets?" Cole asked in a low voice. "No pun intended."

Grace's lips twitched. "Very ingenious, you guys! Keep up the good work and you just might win the grand prize."

"I hope so." Haylie beamed. "Rob used to be a Boy Scout, so we have an advantage." The boy's cheeks turned the same shade of red as the flag above his head when his girlfriend patted his hand. "Good luck to you and Cole, though."

"How is it they know my name but I don't know theirs?" Cole murmured.

"Haylie and Rob attend Pastor Matt's youth group at Church of the Pines."

"I've never attended a service there."

"This is a small town, remember? *Everyone* knows your name."

Cole wasn't sure how he felt about that. If people knew his name, it meant they instantly connected him with Sloan. Even though his grandfather had been born and raised in Mirror Lake, he hadn't been the easiest man to get along with.

Grace had mentioned once that her parents had tried to reach out to Sloan over the years, but he'd never accepted any help.

He'd never offered any either, Cole thought, battling the bitterness that crashed over him every time he remembered the months following his father's death.

Bettina and his brothers had turned to him instead of their mother whenever they needed something. While the guys his age were planning the next senior skip day, Cole had lain awake in bed at night, wondering how he was going to find time to study for his calculus exam when the twins needed help with their science fair project. Bettina barely let him out of her sight, following him from room to room as if she were afraid he would disappear, too.

His father's life insurance policy covered most of the bills, but his mother wasn't able to work, so their modest savings account had slowly dwindled down to nothing as the months slipped away. It had been up to Cole to find a job and help make ends meet.

There hadn't been time for hanging out with his buddies

or going out on a date. It would have taken an understanding woman to share that burden.

Someone with a lot of patience and a sense of humor.

His gaze settled on Grace again.

At seventeen, she'd had both.

She also had plans of her own, Cole reminded himself. *It wouldn't have been fair to ask her to change them for you.*

That's why he hadn't given her the chance.

Chapter Ten

Grace watched a family setting up their lawn chairs a few yards away and tried not to wince. The competition had drawn a fairly good-size crowd of people, but judging from the number of them who'd staked a claim near flag number eight, it was becoming clear that she and Cole were drawing the most attention!

Word must have gotten out that Sloan Merrick's grandson was one of the competitors and they were curious about him....

"You two make a great team!" One of Grace's coworkers shouted.

Or they were more interested in watching the sparks flying between her and Cole than they were in the ones from the campfire.

Grace hiked up the hem of her skirt and lunged toward a stand of trees. "I'll find some kindling."

Cole caught up to her a split second later. "We have to stick together, remember? It's one of the rules."

Had she forgotten? No. Did she want to break that particular rule?

Yes.

Grace scooped up a handful of dry pine needles, all too

aware of Cole. He began to whistle as he picked up sticks and Grace found herself humming along with the familiar tune.

The sun was warm, the air fragrant.

It reminded her of the summer days they'd spent together when Cole had moved to Mirror Lake. They'd explored the woods. Built a campfire near the shore and roasted marshmallows over an open flame.

"Just like old times, isn't it?"

Cole's quiet comment slipped through a crack in Grace's defenses and she sucked in a breath, stunned to discover he'd been thinking the same thing.

"This should be enough." She retreated, ready to face the curiosity of the crowd she'd wanted to avoid rather than face her feelings. Feelings she thought had died a long time ago, but instead, had only been dormant. Waiting to bloom under the warmth of Cole's smile.

He grabbed another stick and followed her back to the campsite.

"You're right. It should be enough to start a fire." Cole dumped the kindling he'd collected into the fire pit. "If we had something to start it *with*."

"Rob and Haylie bartered with Jenna and Dev for the flint, but we don't have anything to trade except our tarp." Grace chewed on her bottom lip. "I thought we'd use that to make the shelter."

"I have an apple in my car." Cole was already striding away. "Let's try that."

Grace ducked her head, but not before Cole saw her smile. It gave him the courage to reach for her hand again.

So she wouldn't stumble over one of the roots protruding from the worn footpath.

They sprinted through the grass to the parking lot, but no one seemed too concerned about their destination. Cole opened the door of the backseat and grabbed a white paper sack. "Iola stopped at a farmer's market on her way to work yesterday morning. She was worried I'd forget to eat breakfast."

Grace peeked inside and her eyes went wide.

"This isn't breakfast. I'm not even sure it's an apple."

"There's supposed to be one. Underneath the layer of chocolate. And the caramel."

"And the pecans." Grace rolled the top of the bag shut. "And you thought Skittles would get us disqualified. I'm pretty sure caramel apples like this didn't exist in 1887."

"We don't know that for sure. And everything on it can be found in nature," Cole pointed out.

"Except the sprinkles."

He grinned. "The important thing is, do you think we can convince Jenna and Dev to trade their flint for it?"

His heart went into a freefall when Grace grinned back.

"Oh, I think we can do better than that."

They stumbled into the couple's campsite a few minutes later. Jenna was mixing something up in a wooden bowl and Dev was in the process of rigging up a tripod, consisting of a metal grate and stones, over the fire.

Grace hadn't been exaggerating. The guy did have skills.

"Flapjack batter," Jenna announced. "At least, that's what it's supposed to be. Right now, it looks more like paste."

Which meant they were already working on the second part of the challenge.

"You want the flint, don't you?" Dev asked.

To his astonishment, Grace shook her head. "We don't have time to start one. We need some of those." She pointed to sticks crackling in the fire ring.

Dev and Jenna exchanged an incredulous look.

"You want us to give you *fire?*"

"We want to trade it. For this." Grace pulled the caramel apple out of the sack and held it up like a trophy.

Dev frowned. "Is that—"

Jenna was already reaching for it. "You heard her, sweetheart."

"You realize this is going to give them an edge." Dev gave Grace a friendly wink to let her know he was teasing.

"We either offer this apple to the judge or one of my flapjacks," Jenna told him.

Dev stepped away from the circle of stones and made a sweeping gesture at the campfire.

"Take whatever you need."

"We have fire!"

Much to the crowd's delight—and Grace's embarrassment—Cole lifted her right off her feet and swung her around.

Someone held up a hand-lettered sign with the words *Team Eight* written on it in bright green crayon.

"Don't let that go to your head, guys!" Kate shouted.

"We'll be humble winners," Cole called back as he set Grace down again. "I promise."

"You're only encouraging her, you know."

"Encouraging her to what?"

Matchmake, Grace wanted to howl.

Who knew what her friends were thinking? Or plotting? Grace had a feeling they would try to convince Cole to attend the fireworks later that night at the inn.

The last time she and Cole had watched a fireworks display together had been at the Fourth of July celebration the summer they'd met. They'd shared a blanket and a package of Skittles. And a kiss that had curled her bare toes....

"Ready for challenge number two?" Cole reached out his hand.

When people started to applaud and whistle, Grace had no choice but to take his hand.

"That wasn't so bad, was it?" he whispered.

"No." Not bad at all, Grace thought.

That was the trouble.

Esther waved to Grace as she and Cole sprinted past the Redstones' campsite. The aroma of some concoction drifted from their campfire.

"Something tells me that whatever she's cooking is going to taste better than Jenna and Dev's flapjacks," Cole muttered.

The general store was vacant when they skidded up to it.

"Ms. McAllister!" Grace called out. "Faye?"

Cole picked up a wooden spoon and started to bang on the bottom of a copper pot.

"I'm not deaf!" Faye was stalking toward them, a very modern fire extinguisher tucked under one arm. "Quinn and Abby ran into a little…trouble…and I had to give them a hand."

Cole grinned. "That's—" he let out a grunt when Grace stepped on his foot "—a shame."

"We're ready for the breakfast challenge," she said.

Faye pulled some envelopes from her apron pocket and let them choose one. Cole leaned in close as Grace tore it open and pulled out a slip of paper.

"Omelet." Grace couldn't help but smile. "That won't be too difficult. I make them all the time at home."

"I'll be at your campsite in ten minutes. Use three eggs. All this fresh air is making me hungry." Faye turned to walk away.

"Wait a second!" Grace called. "Where *are* the eggs?"

"I imagine they're with the chickens."

Grace and Cole exchanged a look.

"And that would be—"

"Somewhere in the park," came the cheerful response. "Eddie and I let the hens loose about five o'clock this morning."

Meaning they had to *find* the eggs.

It was official: Mayor Dodd had a wicked sense of humor.

"This is crazy," Cole protested. "How are we supposed to find a flock of chickens? It's not like they come when you call them."

Grace's eyes lit up.

"One of them does." She grabbed his hand. "Come on."

Cole didn't protest. Not because he believed that Grace was some kind of modern-day bird whisperer, but because this was the first time he sensed there might be a crack in the invisible wall she had put up between them.

She towed him toward the opposite end of the park.

"My friend Emma Sutton is the librarian, and last week Eddie brought Peggy Lee, one of his chickens, to story hour because they were reading *Charlotte's Web*. It was the only farm animal she could find on short notice." Grace paused to take a breath. "Anyway, Emma mentioned that Peggy Lee would come right up to Charlie when he whistled the first line of…of one of the old songs the *real* Peggy Lee was famous for."

"What old song?"

"Fever."

Cole stared at her. "This town should have its own reality show."

Grace didn't disagree. "If we hurry, we'll be in second place. Daniel and Esther haven't started building their shelter yet."

They still had a chance to win the competition. The grand prize, a romantic dinner for two.

Would Grace go with him?

Mayor Dodd had mentioned that Abby O'Halloran was

going to host it next Saturday. He could always come back to Mirror Lake for the weekend. Finish up another project.

See Grace again.

She began to whistle a familiar tune, one Cole remembered hearing on the oldies station that blared from the speakers in Cap's office.

"I don't think—"

"Shh." Grace stopped. "Did you hear something?"

"Other than the people over there laughing hysterically?"

"I tried to warn you that you didn't know what you were getting into." Grace started whistling again.

Cole felt a tug in the general vicinity of his heart.

No, he hadn't known what he was getting into. Because he hadn't counted on Grace.

He was supposed to meet with the lawyer to determine the exact specifications of the will and then leave the house and land in a Realtor's capable hands. Return to Madison and wait for a phone call while he talked to the bank about buying another plane.

Nothing had gone according to plan.

At the moment, watching Grace's slim shoulders sway in time with the beat, he didn't mind.

"I heard a cackle." Grace picked up her skirts, sprinted toward a hedge near the pump.

A large chicken with butter-colored feathers and a fancy white crest on top of its head strutted into view.

Cole couldn't believe it.

"We found her!"

"That's not all we found." Cole spotted two brown eggs lying in a shallow depression a foot away from the hen.

He took a step closer, but Grace grabbed his arm.

"Wait a second. I just remembered something else Emma said about Peggy Lee."

Cole paused. "Okay."

"She bites."

"Chickens don't have teeth, Grace. I don't think they bite."

Grace didn't look too sure.

"I'll be all—"

Two things happened at the same time. Cole reached for the egg and Peggy Lee reached for *him*.

The hen doubled in size and beat her wings and…charged.

Cole yelped.

Okay, maybe not teeth, but definitely a beak like an ice pick.

He scuttled backward to escape and tripped. Of course. Because running away from a chicken wasn't enough to lose his man card.

Peggy Lee continued to advance, wings lifted like a sheriff in a cheesy Western flick, ready to draw on him.

"Get the eggs while I think of a way to distract her," he told Grace.

"It looks like you're already doing a pretty good job of that." Her voice sounded strange. Muffled.

Cole slid a quick look at her—careful to keep an eye trained on Peggy Lee.

Grace's hands were covering her face and she was doubled over.

It took a moment for him to realize she was…laughing.

At him, not the chicken.

Rising to his feet, Cole ruefully acknowledged to himself that he'd wanted to hear Grace laugh.

At least he'd succeeded at one of the challenges.

Chapter Eleven

"It wasn't *that* funny."

Cole shot her a wry look and Grace realized he'd caught her again. She caught her lower lip between her teeth to stop her smile from spreading.

"It was very clever of you to distract Peggy Lee while I retrieved the eggs."

"Uh-huh." Cole's voice was dry. "Do you think that will be the caption posted along with the video clip? I saw at least a dozen cell phones pointed in our direction."

Grace had seen Wes Collins, the editor of the *Mirror Lake Register,* snapping pictures, too, but decided not to mention that. Maybe she could convince him not to put it on the front page of next week's edition.

"You wouldn't begrudge Peggy Lee her sixty seconds of fame, would you?" she teased.

"I can see the headline now. *Which one is the chicken?*" Cole chuckled. "But it's not like you didn't warn me."

The butterflies that had taken up residence in Grace's stomach stirred. As if they hadn't been performing a whole repertoire of impressive dives, barrel rolls and loop-the-loops since Cole had shown up at her front door that morning.

"Anything else I should know?"

I don't want you to leave tomorrow.

Grace stole a look at Cole and their eyes met. There was laughter in his cedar-green eyes and something else. Something that made her heart bump against her ribs.

"No." The word stuck in her throat.

Cole went back to scrubbing out the skillet with water and a handful of sand. Faye had trudged down to their campsite to taste the omelet, garnished with a handful of chives they'd found growing in one of the flower beds at the entrance of the park. She'd chewed several times and marked something down on her clipboard.

Of course she wouldn't announce their score, but Grace saw the woman surreptitiously pull a Snickers bar out of her apron pocket when she was walking away.

"We've got about half an hour. Maybe a little less." Cole kicked sand over the fire to douse the rest of the flames. "I suppose we better get started on the shelter."

Because Cole had an agenda and nothing was going to change that.

As soon as the competition was over, Grace reminded herself, he would go back to his grandfather's house and start fixing it up. Not for himself, but for someone else. If he'd had any sentimental attachment to the town, he would have come back long before now.

"We can use the tarp as a roof, but we should probably find something else for the walls. Do you think we're going to be judged on whether it's structurally sound?"

"If we are, the Redstones are going to have the advantage again. Daniel is a carpenter." Grace swatted a mosquito that had found a patch of exposed skin below her ear.

Cole was already wading into the thick stand of trees that formed a hedge around their camp. "A carpenter. It figures."

"So is Quinn O'Halloran, Abby's husband, but it's more

of a hobby for him." Grace couldn't prevent a smile when she remembered the way the couple had met.

Abby's brother, Alex, had secretly hired Quinn, a marine and former bodyguard, to keep an eye on his sister while she turned the old Bible camp on the shore of Mirror Lake into a quaint bed-and-breakfast.

Alex hadn't been happy when Quinn and Abby fell in love. He'd shown up in Mirror Lake for the wedding—and fallen head over heels for Kate Nichols.

Grace was thrilled for her friends, but she couldn't help but feel a little envious at the same time.

Especially when the men in their lives had decided to make their home in Mirror Lake.

The town Cole couldn't wait to leave.

Even though Cole couldn't see Grace, he was all too aware of her as she followed him into the woods to find something they could use to build a shelter.

She was constantly tipping him off balance. Keeping a polite distance between them one minute, teasing him the next. With her words…and the shy glances she cast in his direction.

Maybe she wasn't as indifferent to him as he'd first believed.

Or maybe it was simply wishful thinking on his part.

"There's a tree over there that might work." Grace was beside him now, pointing to a birch that had probably fallen during a storm. She'd taken off the bonnet and drops of sunlight splashed through the leaves in the trees, casting a halo around her hair. The top of her head was almost level with Cole's shoulder, something that had made it easy for him to plant a kiss on her temple when they'd walked together in the woods that long ago summer.

His gaze lingered on the spot.

And the toe of his shoe got caught in a skein of wild grapevine. The ground rushed up to meet him as he pitched forward.

Grace grabbed his arm, but in the process of trying to help, she almost went down with him. They teetered back and forth in an attempt to regain their balance. It was like trying to stay on his feet while playing Twister, one of his sister's favorite games.

Laughing, Grace broke free, her cheeks flushed with color.

For a moment, Cole let himself wonder what life would have been like if he'd come back for her. But keeping his promise to Grace would have forced him to break another one he'd made. To his family.

And it would have changed Grace's future, too.

"I'm sorry." For a lot of things, Cole thought.

"You didn't see that gigantic root sticking out of the ground, mmm?" Grace hiked an eyebrow. "What were you looking at?"

You, Cole was tempted to admit.

"First I get attacked by a chicken and then you have to keep me from falling flat on my face," he said lightly. "At least no one got that on video."

Cole heard a muffled laugh, only this time it wasn't Grace. He looked over his shoulder just in time to see someone disappear behind a birch tree.

Grace had spotted him, too. "Hello, Jeremy. Cody."

Silence. And then, not one, but two adolescent boys slunk into the clearing, hands sunk into the pockets of their cargo shorts.

"Alex hired you to check up on us, didn't he?"

"Nope." The boy with a shock of shaggy wheat-blond hair flashed a sheepish smile. "He asked us to provide him with an update."

Cole believed him. It sounded like something Porter would say.

"I see." Grace ruffled the boy's hair and then brushed away a leaf that clung to his shoulder. He stiffened and Cole assumed he was embarrassed by the attention. "You tell Alex we're going to set a new record for building a shelter. Or—" her eyes twinkled as she continued "—we could always take over the tree fort you and Jeremy built last summer. We'd win the grand prize for sure."

The boys shifted their feet self-consciously, but the wide grins that spread across their faces reflected how pleased they were by the compliment.

Grace smiled at Cole as she made the introductions. "This is Cody Lang and Jeremy Sutton, Emma and Jake's son. Boys, this is Cole Merrick. He's—" Cole waited when she paused, wondering how she was going to finish the sentence "—in town for the weekend."

Cole exhaled slowly, not realizing he'd been holding his breath.

What had he expected?

"It's nice to meet you, Mr. Merrick." To Cole's surprise, both boys stepped forward to shake his hand.

He smiled. "Same here."

The boys exchanged a look.

"We're sorry for sneaking up on you," Jeremy finally mumbled.

"Apology accepted," Grace said. "But you let Alex know that surveillance is against the rules, okay?"

"Okay."

A smile teased the corner of Grace's lips as she watched the boys charge back into the woods to pass on the message. The expression on her face reminded Cole of the one he'd seen when she'd introduced him to Logan and Tori Gardner earlier that morning.

"He's one of yours, right?"

Grace's head snapped around. "What?"

"Cody. He's one of yours."

"How did you know?" Grace regarded him warily, as if he'd uncovered a secret she'd been trying to keep.

"The way you fussed over him. The look in your eyes."

"What look?"

"Affection. Concern. Pride." Cole had seen all those things.

She was silent for a moment. "You're right. I'm not Cody's caseworker, but I met him when I helped his mother, Renée, get the paperwork in order so she could take classes through the university system."

"And you've been keeping an eye on him ever since," Cole guessed.

"I'm not the only one. In the past few years, the church I attend has taken Cody under their wing. His older brothers have always been a handful, so Renée spends most of her energy trying to keep them out of trouble." There was no undercurrent of judgment or disapproval in Grace's tone. "It's a full-time job, plus she works nights at an assisted living facility about half an hour away, so she has to sleep during the day."

"Leaving Cody to his own devices."

"We're blessed to have a mentoring ministry through Church of the Pines, and Quinn spends a lot of time with Cody one on one. They've both been a great influence on him. I've been talking to Zoey about starting one for girls, too…" Grace stopped. "I'm sorry. I'm sure you aren't interested in this."

"I *am* interested," Cole said slowly. "It sounds like a great program."

"It's more than that. It's a ministry. Quinn had a rough home life when he was growing up, so he understands what

Cody is going through. Renée does the best she can, but most days she's exhausted and that's where Quinn steps in to help. The guys in the mentoring ministry do more than just take the boys out for ice cream or shoot baskets. They pray for them and with them."

It occurred to Cole that he should have looked into something like that for Sean and Travis when they were Cody's age. A lot of times he'd been at his wit's end, trying to be both father and older brother to preteen boys who loved to push the boundaries.

But as the oldest, Cole was the head of the family. He had been determined to handle things without outside help.

He couldn't run the risk they'd lose their mother, too.

"Cody isn't considered at-risk, but a lot of children like him eventually end up in the foster care system. Fortunately, some of them are adopted into stable, loving homes."

"Like Logan and Tori."

Grace's widened a little, as if she were surprised he had realized who she was talking about. "Sometimes all the children need is someone who has the courage to say yes. It doesn't mean it won't be difficult. It doesn't mean a person won't have to make sacrifices. But…it's worth it." She gave a little laugh. "Sorry. I'm stepping down from my soapbox now."

"They're lucky to have someone like you on their side," Cole said quietly. "I'm sure there are more kids who need homes than people who are willing to provide them."

Grace drew in a breath, shaken by the statement. She hadn't planned to have this conversation, not with Cole. But more than that, she hadn't expected him to understand. To see the genuine compassion in his eyes when she'd told him about Cody's situation.

What would he say if she told him that she'd already been approved by a private adoption agency? She'd kept that information a secret for almost a year, but suddenly, Grace wanted to share it. With Cole.

"I've been—"

The words she was about to say were drowned out by a commotion behind them. Abby emerged from the woods with Quinn at her side. Kate and Alex were right behind them.

"Those boys gave away our location," she heard Cole mutter.

"We thought we heard voices!" Abby said cheerfully. "How is your shelter coming along?"

Grace felt the color rise in her cheeks.

That's right. They were supposed to be working on the final challenge.

"We got a little…sidetracked," she murmured.

"Uh-huh." Kate smiled at Cole. "I can see how that might happen."

"Are you almost finished with yours?"

"Well…" Abby tucked her arm through her husband's. "We were slowed down by a situation beyond our control. Fortunately, Faye came to our rescue with a fire extinguisher."

"We had one of those…situations…too." Grace struggled to keep a straight face.

Abby looked at Cole and grinned. "Yeah, we heard about that."

"Keep in mind the stories have been grossly exaggerated," he said.

"Stories?" There was a gleam of laughter in Quinn's eyes. "One of the boys in Matt's youth group showed us the video."

Cole nudged Grace's arm. "What did I tell you?" he whispered.

"I don't think any of us are going to make the deadline." Kate sighed. "We've got what…half an hour left? And Alex gave our hatchet to Rob and Haylie."

"The kid was trying to cut through branches with a Swiss Army knife," Porter said drily. "He would have lopped off a finger, and then I would have had to bandage him up."

Kate went up on her tiptoes and kissed his cheek. "You are such a softie."

To Cole's amazement, Porter smiled.

"This one looks good." Quinn was studying the birch sapling. "It's about the right size."

It was also the one he and Grace had had their eye on.

"I don't know how the mayor expects us to complete all these challenges when we're allowed only one item," Kate huffed.

"One of which happens to be a coffeepot," Quinn said under his breath.

"It called to me. I forgot we didn't have any coffee to put in it."

Abby poked him in the side with her elbow and Quinn winked at her.

Watching the couple interact, the love that shimmered in the air between them, Grace felt that familiar pinch of envy. For those few moments, when she and Cole had laughed together and he had listened so intently while she shared her heart, it would have been all too easy to fool herself into thinking they were a couple again.

But Grace wasn't about to make the same mistake twice.

"Hey!" Emma stood on the trail, shielding her eyes against the sun. "What's going on? Did you decide to throw a party and forget to invite the rest of us?"

"We're trying to figure out the best way to build a shelter," Kate called back. "With one hatchet. And a coffeepot."

Emma grinned. "Jake and I have a roll of twine."

The best way.

Grace realized she'd said the words out loud when Kate's

gaze cut back to her. "What are you thinking?" she demanded.

"I think—" Abby moved closer, a smile spreading across her face "—Grace is thinking the same thing *I'm* thinking."

"Here we go." Alex looked up at the heavens, as if appealing for help.

Quinn shrugged. "I'm in."

"Jake and I will tell the rest of the group." Emma turned around and started back down the path.

"Tell them what?"

Grace saw the confused look on Cole's face and almost felt sorry for him. "There's been a slight change in plans."

"We're going to put our own, to use the mayor's term, *unique,* spin on the shelter," Kate added.

Cole looked at Grace for a translation.

"We're still going to build a shelter, but it's going to be big enough for all of us. And we're going to pool our resources and build it together."

As if on cue, the rest of the couples began to show up.

"Okay, people!" Kate hopped up on a tree stump. "We've got less than an hour. Guys, start looking for downed trees. The girls will collect branches. We can put them over Cole and Grace's tarp to make a roof."

"Are you sure this is okay?" Haylie Owens cast a worried look at the older adults in the circle. "I mean, the mayor didn't say we could work together."

"No, but he didn't say we couldn't, either." Grace reached out and squeezed the girl's hand. "Two are better than one…"

"Because they have a good return for their work." Haylie finished the rest of the sentence. "That was our memory verse last week!"

"Right." Grace was pleased she remembered. "And I'd say Ecclesiastes 4:9 trumps the mayor's rules. So tell Rob we need your hatchet."

"Haylie has a point," Cole said in a low voice. "Doesn't this defeat the whole purpose of the competition? If we pitch in and build a shelter together, who wins?"

Grace couldn't help but smile at the question.

"All of us."

Chapter Twelve

"It looks like you and Grace are getting along pretty well."

Cole, who'd been tying branches together with the twine that Emma and Jake Sutton had donated to the cause, paused to look up at Kate.

He smiled. "She's been great."

Kate, for once, didn't smile back.

"I talked to Sissy a few minutes ago. She mentioned that you have a meeting with her Monday morning."

It suddenly occurred to Cole that Grace's friend hadn't stopped to make small talk.

He rocked back on his heels. "That's right."

"I didn't realize you'd planned to sell the property."

"Why would I keep it? It's not like I have good memories of the place." Cole regretted the words as soon as they slipped out of his mouth.

Why had he mentioned that? It wasn't as if he and the café owner were friends.

Kate regarded him evenly. "You could make some."

"I have other plans."

"I realize that. Now." Kate glanced over her shoulder and dropped her voice a notch. "We all love Grace. I can't tell you how many families she's helped over the years."

Cole thought of the way Logan and Tori Gardner had run up to Grace and hugged her when they'd arrived at the park earlier that morning. The way Cody had perked up under the warmth of her smile.

"She's good at taking care of people."

"Around here, we take care of each other."

Cole understood.

"The way you're taking care of Grace right now?"

"Yes." Kate didn't look the least bit guilty.

"We're spending a few hours together. That's it." But even as Cole said the words, he wondered if he was being completely honest with himself.

"That's what I'm worried about," Kate said frankly. "You don't know Grace. She doesn't date very much. If anyone even tries to set her up with a friend or a brother or somebody's second cousin, she practically runs screaming in the opposite direction."

Cole might have thought she was exaggerating if he hadn't remembered the conversation he'd overheard between the two men standing next to him at the box social. The guy in the purple tie had mentioned that Grace had turned him down multiple times. She had always been on the shy side, but now she seemed…guarded.

"Grace has always been a private person, but this is different," Kate said, almost as if she'd read his mind. *Scary.* "But we figure some obnoxious jerk broke her heart in college and she isn't in a big hurry to jump into another relationship. Alex and I would hate to see her hurt again."

Cole would have been amused by the warning if he hadn't known that Porter possessed the ways and means—and personality—to make a person's life very uncomfortable if he set his mind to it.

"Grace and I are…teammates." At this point, Cole wasn't even sure if he could claim they were friends.

"Uh-huh." Kate looked skeptical. "I recognize the signs and—"

"What signs?" Cole interrupted.

"You know. She looks at you when you aren't looking. You look at her when she isn't looking. Those kind of signs."

Cole glanced in Grace's direction and saw her deep in conversation with Jenna and Abby. A conversation Kate must have set up to keep Grace distracted until her lecture ended.

Grace's gaze suddenly shifted away from Jenna and locked with his. Across the distance that separated them, he saw her lips curve in a smile, one that warmed Cole from the inside out.

He couldn't help but return it.

"Teammates." Kate rolled her eyes. "Right."

"What are you two talking about?" Grace was suddenly right there in front of him, a bundle of pine boughs cradled in her arms.

Kate didn't miss a beat. "How protective Alex can be when it comes to the people he cares about."

"That's true," Grace said. "Just ask Quinn. And Abby. And Jenna...never mind. There isn't time to list them all."

Cole suppressed a smile, glad to know that Grace had such loyal friends. She belonged here, in Mirror Lake, part of a close-knit community that looked out for one another.

He belonged in Madison.

But suddenly the thought of returning to his empty home, something Cole had patiently waited twelve years for, didn't seem as appealing as it had twenty-four hours ago.

Rob loped past, dragging another log as a group of his friends shouted encouragement. More people had gathered to watch when it became clear the couples had decided to join forces for the final challenge.

Abby O'Halloran had spoken to Faye McAllister and Cole

had seen the woman leading the mayor away from the campsites. He could only assume she'd joined the conspiracy.

As the final minutes ticked by, one of the teenage boys had started shouting out a final countdown.

"Almost finished," Haylie sang out.

"Finally." Alex cuffed Cole on the shoulder as he strode past. "Then it's back to business as usual."

Cole released a slow breath, knowing he should probably thank the guy for the reminder.

For some reason, Grace couldn't quite meet the mayor's eyes as he walked past her, hands clasped behind his back.

Probably because she felt like a student about to be chastised for not turning in her homework assignment on time.

"I'm not sure how to declare a winner," Mayor Dodd finally said. "Because all of you technically completed the same shelter."

She knew she should probably feel guilty for not following directions, but the feeling of satisfaction that came when she looked at the shelter was stronger.

It had a roof, four walls and a slightly crooked front door. And thanks to Daniel Redstone, it even had a window. On the sill, a delicate breeze ruffled the bouquet of daisies and brown-eyed Susans sprouting from the top of Abby's coffeepot.

Grace thought the flowers were a particularly nice touch.

"I wasn't expecting my contestants to break the rules, but—" Mayor Dodd's mustache twitched "—I should have known it would happen. Because the same thing happened a hundred and twenty-five years ago.

"The people who settled Mirror Lake were strong. Creative. Disciplined. Independent. But they also knew when to lean on each other, the way everyone did today. That's the reason they were successful. It's the reason our little town thrived. It's the reason it continues to thrive."

Tears misted Grace's eyes, and she found herself wishing she'd worn her bonnet.

Maybe no one would notice...

A warm hand wrapped around hers.

Cole had noticed. Which only caused the pressure against the back of her eyes to increase.

"Now then." The mayor tugged at the brim of his hat. "Esther and Daniel Redstone were the winners of the breakfast competition and will receive a brand-new cast-iron skillet, a generous donation from our local hardware store." He waited for the applause to die down. "The grand prize for today's competition, a romantic dinner for two at Abby's bed-and-breakfast, was supposed to be awarded to the couple who finished all three challenges first. Unfortunately—" he frowned down at them, but there was no mistaking the twinkle in his eyes "—it looks like I will have to offer an alternative prize instead, because there are obviously more than two winners."

A collective groan of disappointment rose from the ranks.

"Wait a second!" Kate stepped out of line and flew to the man's side. The mayor angled his head while she whispered something in his ear.

When Kate returned to her place next to Alex, she was smiling.

"I have just been informed it will be dinner for sixteen. Next Saturday night."

Applause erupted around them, but Grace couldn't look at Cole. She was sure he'd rather have an oil change or even an ice-cream cone. Because he wouldn't be in Mirror Lake next weekend.

If the sale of the property went through as quickly as he hoped, he wouldn't be coming back at all.

* * *

A dinner date.

Cole glanced at Grace, but she was putting on the bonnet again, her head bent while she fussed with the strings so he couldn't read her expression.

"You're all invited to join us at Abby's bed-and-breakfast at five o'clock for games and an old-fashioned ice-cream social, followed by fireworks at dusk," the mayor added. "I'll see you there!"

"I guess this is where we part ways. I have to hitch B.C. up for the one-o'clock tour," Grace said, so quickly that it sounded as if she'd rehearsed the words.

"We came together," Cole reminded her, "in my car."

"Kate invited me to have lunch with her and Alex. She offered to drive me home."

Of course. Now that Kate had discovered he wasn't planning to stick around Mirror Lake, she wanted to keep him as far from Grace as possible.

Cole wasn't sure whether to be annoyed or appreciative.

He took the high road and chose door number two. But it didn't stop him from lingering a moment, giving Grace the opportunity to invite him to join her and her friends for lunch.

"I'll make sure no one disturbs you when we tour the cabin and the property. I know you have a lot of work to do."

Yes, he did. And the sooner he finished it, the better.

"I'll see you later, then."

Grace didn't respond, proof that she planned to keep her distance now that the competition was officially over.

"Congratulations!"

Cole turned toward the lilting voice, grateful for the interruption. One more second and he would have said something stupid. Like, "Are you going to the fireworks tonight?" Followed by, "Do you want to go with *me?*"

A couple was walking toward them, hand in hand. The woman broke away from her companion long enough to reel Grace in for a quick hug and then turned to Cole.

"You're still here," she announced. "I shouldn't be surprised, though. That seems to happen a lot."

Behind him, Cole thought he heard Grace…squeak.

He tried to match a name to the face. "Zoey, right?"

"You have a good memory."

Sometimes too good, Cole thought ruefully. He wasn't sure if it was the sweet fragrance of the summer morning, the familiar surroundings or spending a few hours in Grace's company. But whatever it was, he was beginning to feel as if he'd fallen through a crack in time.

If you aren't careful, that's not all you'll be falling for.

He did his best to ignore the teasing inner voice.

"This is my husband, Matthew." Zoey linked arms with the man standing patiently at her side. "Matt, Cole Merrick."

"Cole." Matt reached out and gripped his hand. "I've heard a lot about you."

"Really?" Cole cast a sideways glance at Grace. Twin spots of color rose in her cheeks like flags.

"From your grandfather." To his credit, Matt didn't crack a smile. "I was given the opportunity to get to know Sloan while he was in the hospital."

Cole thought that was a strange way to put it.

"You're a doctor?"

"Pastor."

Cole frowned. Sloan had been deeply suspicious of people who talked openly about things like faith. And new beginnings.

He had discovered that information the hard way when he'd written his grandfather a letter several months after his family left Mirror Lake. Taking Grace's words about forgiveness to heart, Cole decided that holding on to bitterness would only drain the energy he needed to take care of his sister and brothers. The letter had been one more attempt to make things right. To honor his father's memory.

It had been returned a few days later, unopened.

"Matt's the one who started the mentoring ministry I told you about." Grace joined the conversation for the first time.

"It was God's idea," Matt said with an easy smile. "We just listened, took notes and did what He said."

"From what Grace told me, it's helped a lot of kids."

The pastor regarded him thoughtfully. "We're always looking for volunteers."

"Cole isn't staying in Mirror Lake," Grace said. "He's only here to meet with Sissy about selling a piece of property."

A few days ago, when Iola had found the letter from Kate, Cole had been convinced that was the only reason God had brought him to Mirror Lake. But over the past few hours, things had gotten a little confusing.

The feelings Grace stirred inside him were confusing.

Matt's smiled faded a little. "You already decided to sell?"

Why, Cole thought irritably, was everyone so surprised by his decision?

He waited to see if Grace would jump into the conversation again. But no, this time it appeared she was going to let him have the honor of explaining.

"Yes." It was the only thing he could say without launching into a list of reasons he didn't plan to keep his grandfather's home.

A list he couldn't come up with at the moment.

An awkward silence descended.

"We're having an open-air service at the bed-and-breakfast tomorrow morning at nine o'clock." Zoey tried to jumpstart the conversation with a warm smile. "You're more than welcome to join us, Cole."

Cole glanced at Grace. "Do I escort you there, too?"

Zoey chuckled, but even though Grace smiled, it didn't quite reach her eyes.

"No," she murmured. "That's one thing we aren't obligated to attend together."

It wasn't the first time Grace had used that particular word but somehow, it no longer described the way he was feeling.

And if that wasn't enough of a reason to politely decline Zoey and Matt's invitation, he didn't know what was.

"Thanks," he heard himself say. "I'll be there."

Chapter Thirteen

"The Merrick homestead is our final stop on today's tour."

Grace made the announcement as B.C. lumbered up the gravel driveway for the second time that afternoon. The tours had proven to be extremely popular with the locals as well as the tourists.

Ten people, a mixture of all ages, had clambered into the wagon when she'd stopped in front of the bank. Several of the tourists had even asked if she would pose for a photograph.

The lively tour groups would have taken Grace's mind off Cole…if she hadn't been obligated to recite his family history every single time.

With an inward sigh, she launched into the speech she'd prepared the night before.

"Samuel Merrick was twenty-two years old when he built the original cabin and it's still standing today. He worked for a large lumber company, and his boss sent him here to survey the land.

"Samuel and Jeremiah Stone, his best friend, bought up a lot of the property around the lake as an investment. Jeremiah was more interested in harvesting the timber and moving on, but Samuel fell in love with the area…and Ivy Meade, the daughter of a local missionary to the Chippewa Indians.

"The couple decided to stay here and they are considered the first permanent settlers. Samuel's initial investment yielded dividends he never expected. He built the first church. The first school."

All the information Grace shared was part of the speech she'd memorized. A brief overview of the things she'd learned about the homestead before she'd known it would be included in the tour.

What she hadn't realized was that researching the history of the town was the equivalent of researching the Merrick family. The two were so intertwined; there was no way to separate them.

She also hadn't anticipated that the details she'd dedicated to memory would take on a whole new meaning.

The people she was talking about were Cole's family. The things they'd built *his* legacy. She'd even unearthed a faded portrait of Samuel and Ivy on their wedding day in the archives at the local historical society. The couple had dared to break the current tradition by smiling for the photographer.

Grace had thought about showing it to Cole, but didn't think he would be interested. He'd offered no excuses, or apologies, when Matt had questioned his decision to sell the property.

And yet he'd accepted their invitation to attend the worship service in the morning.

Was it possible he was a believer now?

Grace's throat tightened at the thought.

Cole had been so grief-stricken after his father's death, so angry over the way Sloan continued to treat his family, he had told her that he didn't think God cared about him.

But Grace knew He did. So she'd shared passages of scripture. Prayed for him.

And she'd continued to pray even after he'd left town.

Her desire for Cole to know the truth was stronger than the hurt she felt over the way things had ended between them.

"I have a question!"

The teenaged girl who'd been grumbling ever since the last stop leaned forward and tapped Grace on the shoulder. "How old were Samuel and Ivy when they got married?"

It felt like a trick question, but Grace answered honestly, knowing there were facts to back up her answer.

"Ivy was seventeen, and Samuel was twenty-three."

The girl looked at her mother. "See?"

"Things were different in the 1800s, sweetie." The woman shot Grace an exasperated look, as if she were the one who'd given the young couple permission to marry.

"I'm sure Samuel and Ivy were very mature for their age." Grace tried to keep a straight face. "Ivy was the first schoolteacher in Mirror Lake, and she convinced her widowed father to serve as the church's first pastor."

"Which church did he build?" someone asked. "That cute little white one near the park?"

"Church of the Pines." Grace nodded. "Although there were a lot more pine trees when it got its name." She pulled back on the reins as the house came into view. "We have permission to tour the grounds and go into the cabin today, but I would like everyone to please stay together."

Cole's SUV was parked behind the house, but other than that, there had been no sign of him when Grace had taken the first tour group through after lunch.

"Does anyone in the Merrick family live here now?" a woman wearing a bright pink visor asked as she hopped down from the wagon.

"Sloan Merrick died several years ago, and the house has been vacant ever since."

"Then what is *he* doing here?" The woman lowered her

rhinestone glasses and pointed to a familiar figure striding around the side of the house, a tool belt slung low on his hips.

Some questions were easier to answer than others, Grace thought.

"He's fixing a few things around the house before it goes up for sale."

Hopefully, the more she said the words, the more she would believe them.

And the less they would hurt.

Cole yanked out a handful of weeds growing along the foundation of the house and almost ended up falling on his backside.

Wouldn't that be an interesting addition to Grace's tour?

His gaze drifted to the cabin, where the woman he couldn't seem to stop thinking about stood in the doorway of the cabin, one hand resting on the shoulder of a red-haired girl in a bright yellow sundress. Even in the wilting heat, Grace managed to look as fresh as the bouquet of daisies she held in her other hand.

Almost as if she sensed that she was being watched, Grace suddenly turned her head in his direction.

The air emptied out of Cole's lungs.

He hadn't considered the possibility that he would feel anything more than simple nostalgia for the friendship they'd shared that summer. He hadn't expected the years would have added layers to Grace's personality, making her even more attractive.

She was physically beautiful, no doubt about it, but she was also sweet and funny and had a generous, giving heart.

And he was totally attracted to her.

So where did that leave him?

Leave *them*?

Cole closed his eyes and a prayer tumbled out with his sigh.

Lord, I have no idea what I'm supposed to do here. I could use a little help.

Lots of help, actually.

Cole was starting to realize that twelve years of being apart hadn't completely extinguished the feelings he'd had for Grace. Unfortunately, Grace hadn't given him any indication that she felt the same way.

Thanks to the obnoxious jerk Kate had told him about.

He wrapped his hand around another patch of weeds and pulled. The last hour had been spent scraping moss and dirt away from what Cole had assumed was an old patio. But the uneven strip of multicolored paving stones he'd uncovered simply ended. Evidence of a project that had never been completed.

A piece of the foundation came up with the roots and crumbled in Cole's hand.

He swept them into the grass and grabbed another bunch.

That's when he noticed the numbers scratched in the rock. 1915.

The cornerstone, with the date the foundation of the house had been set.

He'd overheard some of the things Grace had been saying when he'd walked to the shed to rummage through Sloan's tools. It was obvious she knew more about the Merrick family than he did. She patiently answered questions from the people on the tour, filling in the blanks with names and dates.

But there were a lot of things Cole didn't know. Things he hadn't *wanted* to know because his life—his future—was in Madison. He felt disconnected to the past, but it had never kept him awake at night.

Cole shifted his weight and as he swept aside another layer of dirt and debris, something caught his eye.

A handprint and initials next to a date, pressed into the concrete when it was still wet.

E. M.

Ethan Merrick.

Cole heard his heart pounding in his ears as he carefully aligned his fingers with his father's.

His father had never spoken about his childhood, but Cole had overheard a conversation between his parents once. Ethan had said he'd been glad to get out from under Sloan's control.

But had he felt the same way about leaving Mirror Lake?

A shadow fell across the grass. When Cole turned around, he found himself face-to-face with a little boy. The freckled face was a colorful mosaic of Kool-Aid stains, dirt and a sticky blue residue that looked suspiciously like cotton candy. The boy flashed a gap-toothed grin as he hunkered down beside Cole.

"Did ya find a treasure?"

Cole stared down at his father's handprint.

"Maybe I did."

"Where's Cole?"

Grace tried not to sigh when a pink-tipped cane sank into the ground an inch from the blanket she'd spread on the ground before the fireworks started.

If she heard those words one more time, she was going to jump off the end of Abby's dock and swim back to town. At least it would lower the chances of having to field more questions about Cole's whereabouts.

"I imagine he's still working on Sloan's house." So he could put it on the market as soon as possible.

Delia peered down at her, and Grace tried to hide her emotions with a smile. She must have failed because Delia clucked her tongue.

"You can sit with me and Charlie if you'd like," she offered.

"I appreciate the invitation, but Jenna and Dev already invited me to sit with them." So had Alex and Kate. Emma and Jake. Zoey and Matt.

And everyone else who'd noticed she was sitting alone.

"If you change your mind, we're right over there." Delia pointed to a set of bright yellow Adirondack chairs facing the lake. "Charlie brought a few extra ice-cream bars," she added in a whisper.

"Thanks, Delia."

To Grace's astonishment, Delia patted the top of her head.

"You've got a whole town that loves you, Gracie. You know that, don't you?"

"Of course I do."

But right now, at this moment, Grace couldn't help but wish that someone else did, too.

Delia shuffled away, and Grace tried to focus on the beauty of the lake, letting the sound of laughter and the waves wash over her. The sun winked low in the horizon and a spray of crimson sparks from Quinn's bonfire shot into the air, nature's preshow before the man-made display began.

Grace had changed into her own clothing for the fireworks, grateful to trade in the long dress for comfortable jeans, a green T-shirt and the flannel shirt she'd stolen from her father's closet before her parents had moved to Boston.

She heard the soft thud of footsteps approaching and sent a silent message to the next person on the list who was feeling sorry for her.

Keep going. Keep going.

"Is this seat taken?"

Grace forgot how to breathe when Cole dropped down on the blanket beside her. He extended his hand.

"Hi, I'm Cole Merrick."

Grace blinked. *"What?"*

"That's my name. Cole Merrick."

"I *know* your name."

"Right." He released a slow breath. "But I'm afraid that's all you know."

Grace stared down at Cole's open hand, not sure what kind of game he was playing.

"What are you doing?" she whispered.

"I'm not sure. I'm making this up as I go along. But humor me." Cole smiled and it sent her heart into a free fall. "And you are?"

"Grace Eversea?" Somehow, it came out sounding like a question.

"It's nice to meet you, Grace." Cole took her hand, lightly squeezed her numb, tingling fingers and then let go. "I'm twenty-nine years old. And…single."

Grace choked back a laugh.

Had he really just wiggled his eyebrows? In the fading light, Grace couldn't be sure.

"Your turn," he prompted.

"So am I. Twenty nine," she added quickly.

"And single?"

"Y-yes."

Cole stretched out his long legs and settled back on his elbows. Totally at ease. And so close their arms were touching. Grace could feel the warmth of his skin begin to seep through the worn flannel of her sleeve.

"What do you do for a living, Grace?"

"Social worker." And why was she finding it so difficult to talk in complete sentences?

He waited.

Grace took the hint. "What about you?"

"I'm a pilot. Pretty cool, huh?" He winked at her and Grace felt it all the way down to her toes.

"Cool," she agreed, hoping he didn't realize the effect he was having on her.

"What made you decide to go into social work?"

As far as questions went, it should have been a simple one. But Grace suddenly found herself at a crossroad. She could respond with a simple statement about wanting to make a difference in someone's life...or she could tell the truth.

"I met a boy...when I was a senior in high school." She stared at the lake, unable to look at him. "His dad was a firefighter and he died when the roof of a burning building collapsed. The whole family was devastated, especially his oldest son.

"They moved to Mirror Lake to start over, but his grandfather was bitter and angry. He could have made things better. Loved them through it. But instead, he made things worse because he was trapped in his own grief. I couldn't help the boy's family, but I decided that if I went to college and learned the right tools, I might...I might be able to help someone else's."

Cole was silent for so long that Grace was terrified she'd revealed too much.

She closed her eyes.

Why had she revealed so much?

"Ask me," he finally said.

Grace frowned, not sure what he meant. Cole's hand cupped her jaw and tilted her face toward his until she was looking right into his eyes.

"Ask me why I decided to become a pilot."

"What made you decide to be a pilot?" Grace whispered.

"I met a girl...when I was in high school. She told me that I could do anything. Be anything. And I believed her."

Chapter Fourteen

Grace's eyes darkened with an emotion Cole couldn't identify.

"Then why…" She tried to pull away, but Cole wouldn't let her go. Not this time. He traced the curve of her jaw with his thumb.

"Why did it take me so long to come back?" he asked.

"No." Grace wound one finger around the chain of the necklace she'd retrieved from Faye the moment the competition had ended. "Why did you leave in the first place?"

For the first time, Cole saw the hurt that simmered below the surface.

That's when he realized how he should have greeted her the evening they'd met again.

With an apology.

It didn't seem possible that Grace had thought about him as often as he'd thought about her over the years. He had been so certain she would have forgotten him. Moved on. So sure he'd made the right decision for both of them.

"Sloan and my mom got into an argument the day we left," Cole said slowly. "She never told me what he said to her, but it must have been pretty bad because when I got back to the house, she already had our suitcases packed and in the trunk.

Half an hour later, we were leaving town. She was so upset that I insisted on driving.

"I tried to talk to her, to find out what they'd argued about, but the only thing Mom would say was that Sloan was right." Cole shook his head. "I figured she'd calm down in a few days, but she…got worse." Cole could still remember how helpless he had felt, watching her slip away from them.

"She would get up in the morning and get everyone off to school, but she didn't want to leave the house. Or take care of it. My sister and brothers started coming to me instead of her when they needed something. It was like Mom was going through the motions of living but not really living. I didn't know what to do."

"Did you talk to anyone about it?"

"About halfway through the year, I finally scraped up the courage and told one of my teachers. She said Mom was still grieving and recommended I just give her some space. That 'time heals all wounds.' But time went by, and things didn't change."

Grace wove her fingers through his. "I'm so sorry."

"So was I." Not only had they lost their father, but it felt as if they'd lost their mother, too.

"What did you do?"

"The best I could." Cole shrugged. "I got a part-time job after school to help pay the bills. I loved being around planes and Cap, my boss, needed someone to do all the things he didn't want to do. I talked him into giving me flying lessons instead of a raise and ended up getting my pilot's license. He sold the business to me when he retired a few years ago. It worked out pretty well."

"What about your family?" Grace ventured. "Do they still live with you?"

Cole chuckled. "You'd think so, wouldn't you? Looking at all the stuff they left in my car. Sean and Travis graduated in

May and joined the military together. They're in basic training right now. Bettina went to Scotland for the summer on a study abroad program."

"It sounds like they're doing great."

He heard the question Grace wasn't sure how to ask.

"Mom is, too." Cole smiled. "A few years ago a woman named Lily Donahue started attending our church. I'm not sure why she noticed us, but she started asking questions." Questions he hadn't wanted to answer. "She must have figured out what was going on because she stopped over a lot and spent time with Mom while I was at work. She cornered me in the hangar one day and sat me down for a long talk. Straightened me out about a few things."

"That depression isn't something to be ashamed of?" Grace asked softly.

Cole should have known she would understand.

"Lily had struggled with it for years before she admitted she needed help," Cole said. "She wasn't afraid to reach out to Mom. To encourage her to see a doctor. Something I should have done."

"You were barely eighteen years old, Cole. You can't beat yourself up about that. You didn't understand what was happening and you were dealing with your own grief."

"Lily said the same thing. But it wasn't only that," he admitted. "I was afraid if someone outside the family got involved, my brothers and sister would get taken away. I knew Dad would have wanted me to take care of them. So I did."

But who took care of you?
The words trembled on Grace's lips even though she already knew the answer to that question.

Cole hadn't done the best he could. He'd done everything. Taken care of his three younger siblings. Kept the household in order. Watched over his mother.

But why hadn't he confided in her? Why had he insisted on bearing that burden alone?

"There were times I thought God wasn't listening, but Lily was an answer to prayer," Cole continued. "Eventually, she talked Mom into taking a photography class in the evenings. She'd always liked taking pictures, and Lily thought it might be a good way to help her re-engage." A mysterious smile touched Cole's lips. "She was right."

"She made some friends," Grace guessed.

"You could say that. George Wilke, the instructor, noticed Mom had a natural talent, and he started to spend extra time with her."

"That was nice of him."

"I'm pretty sure he had an ulterior motive." Cole's lips quirked. "As we speak, Mom and George are on a honeymoon cruise to Alaska."

Grace clapped her hand over her mouth. "They got *married?*"

"I walked her down the aisle last month. George is a great guy. Easygoing, and he's got a sense of humor. Mom needs that in her life. They're talking about moving to Arizona in the fall and I have to say, Mom seems excited about leaving Wisconsin winters behind."

"Do you mind?"

"I'll miss them, but for the first time I can concentrate on Painted Skies. I've got a few plans in the works. Things I couldn't do while I split my time and attention between my family and the business."

She heard the excitement in Cole's voice and scraped up a smile.

"Is that why you decided to sell the property now?"

"I didn't know I *owned* the property until I got Kate's letter." Cole raked a hand through his hair. "Yup. You look as stunned as I was when I found out. I won't know all the details until I meet with Mr. Sullivan Monday, but I had no idea Sloan had left everything to me.

"If Kate hadn't written, asking for permission to show people the homestead this weekend, I still wouldn't know. Then Bettina misfiled the letter, and I didn't find it until a few days ago. Iola always says that God's timing is perfect."

"But you...I didn't think you and your grandfather had reconciled."

"Mom and I didn't even know he'd passed away until someone at the funeral home sent us a copy of the obituary. Sloan had requested a private burial, no friends or family. Apparently a condition of the will was that I would only find out about the inheritance if I came back to Mirror Lake on my own."

But he hadn't, Grace thought. Kate's letter had prompted his return. They wouldn't have met again.

Grace was almost afraid to believe that might be part of God's timing, too.

"Grace? I can see the wheels turning. What are you thinking?"

"I understand why you had to leave, but why didn't you tell me? I would have helped, any way I could."

"I know," Cole said softly. "That's why I didn't tell you."

"That doesn't make any..." The rest of the sentence trailed off. "You decided you had to do it on your own, didn't you?"

"My family situation was so complicated...I couldn't drag you into it. You had dreams. Plans. It wouldn't have been fair."

So he'd left without a word. Let her believe she hadn't meant anything to him at all when the opposite had been true.

Cole had protected her, the way he'd protected his family.

Grace didn't know whether to shake him for making a decision without asking what *she* wanted or hug him for being so selfless.

A loud boom shook the air, a signal the fireworks were about to begin.

With a start, Grace realized the sun had gone down. She could barely see the silhouettes of the people around them. What was even more surprising was that none of her friends had interrupted their conversation.

"We're going to have to finish this conversation in about half an hour," she whispered.

"I'm looking forward to it." Cole reached into his shirt pocket. "Here. I figured I owed you one."

Grace laughed when she saw a package of Skittles in his hand.

"I can't believe you remembered this was my favorite candy." She smiled up at him.

"That's not the only thing I remember." Cole's arms slipped around her. Before she realized his intention, he bent down and claimed her lips in a slow, searching kiss. One that brought back memories of their yesterday and hinted at a promise of tomorrow.

When they broke apart a few moments later, Grace had lost the ability to speak.

"I'm sorry, Grace." Cole groaned. "I probably shouldn't have done that."

"No, you shouldn't have."

He looked so upset that Grace lost the battle to keep a straight face. She peek up at him from under her lashes and flashed a mischievous smile. "After all, we just met."

Now it was Cole's turn to look shocked. Then he threw back his head and laughed.

"You don't make a habit of kissing on the first date, do you?" Grace lifted a brow.

She was teasing him again, but Cole's expression turned serious. "I don't make a habit of dating at all. But," he added, "I'm willing to start. I want to see you again, Grace."

* * *

Cole could almost hear the door of Grace's heart slamming shut. He vaulted to his feet and took her by the hand.

"Walk with me. Please."

Fortunately, Grace didn't resist when he veered toward the gardens he'd noticed behind the bed-and-breakfast. Luminaries lined the stone path that wound to the gazebo and Cole was relieved to see that no one else had already claimed it for a quiet conversation. He did want to see her again, but he hadn't meant to blurt it out like that.

He hadn't meant to kiss her, either.

But she'd melted against him, returning the kiss with a sweet passion that had left Cole reeling. And told him that he wasn't the only one who remembered the feelings they'd once had for each other.

He guided her to one of the wicker benches and sat down beside her.

"I want to see you again," he repeated.

She averted her gaze. "I'm not sure that's a good idea."

"Look, I know someone hurt you—"

"What?"

"Kate…she mentioned you'd been hurt by some obnoxious jerk in the past, and it's made you cautious."

Grace made a strangled sound that could have been a laugh or a sob. She started to rise to her feet and Cole put his hand on hers. The contact sparked that familiar jolt of electricity. He heard Grace pull in a breath and knew she'd felt it, too.

"I didn't expect to feel this way either," he admitted in a low voice. "All I'm asking is that you give us a chance."

"I already did."

He stared down at her, trying to make sense out of the quiet statement. And when he did, the truth smacked him upside the head.

"*I'm* the obnoxious jerk."

He saw the truth reflected in her eyes.

"You were young," Grace finally said. "We were *both* young. When you left and never contacted me again, I thought it meant you'd lied to me. That we had a summer romance and when summer was over…so were we."

Cole closed his eyes.

A summer romance? If anything, the depth of his feelings for Grace had scared him to death. He'd fallen in love with her. It hadn't been easy to sever their relationship. The only reason he'd done it was because he believed it was ultimately for the best.

Now he wasn't sure.

"I'm an obnoxious jerk *and* an idiot, Grace."

Grace smiled but didn't deny it. She did, however, let him off the hook because that's the kind of person she was.

"It was a long time ago. And in spite of what Kate or anyone else thinks, I don't expect you to ask me to the homecoming dance."

Her attempt at humor made Cole feel even worse.

"What about dinner?"

She looked away and he hated to see the uncertainty in her eyes.

"You're leaving."

The words hung in the air between them.

"Have dinner with me next Saturday night."

"You're coming back next weekend?"

He was now.

"We won the competition, remember? We have to claim the grand prize." He winked at her. "Along with seven other couples."

Grace was tempted to pinch herself, just to make sure she wasn't dreaming.

Cole wanted to see her again.

Equal parts of hope and panic collided.

"I'd like that," she heard herself say.

"Should I swing by in the morning and pick you up for church?"

"I promised Abby I'd be at the inn an hour early to help set up the refreshments for the fellowship time after the service."

"Okay. I'll catch up with you there."

She nodded, knowing that if she tried to say something, she would only end up stuttering like a girl on her first date.

"We can make this work." Cole leaned over and sealed the promise with another lingering kiss.

It took all Grace's self-control not to cling to him. As it was, she practically floated home. The evening had started out with her sitting alone...and ended with her in Cole's arms.

Is this part of Your plan, Lord?

Was it possible that after twelve years, she and Cole were being given a second chance?

As Grace unlocked the front door, her cell phone vibrated in her pocket. It was probably her parents, curious to find out how the tours had gone.

"Hello?" She sat down on the bottom step and tugged off one of her boots.

"I hope I didn't wake you."

"Hi, Meredith." Grace recognized the adoption agency director's clipped, no-nonsense voice immediately. "And no, I wasn't asleep. I just got home from the fireworks." An image of Cole holding her in his arms flashed through her mind. Grace was glad the woman couldn't see her blush.

"Oh, that's right. Mirror Lake's one hundred and twenty-fifth birthday celebration." Amusement flowed below the words now. "How could I have forgotten?"

Grace was reminded of something *she* had forgotten. An email Meredith had sent to her earlier in the week.

"I'm sorry I didn't get back to you sooner with details about the spring seminar. I took a few days off from work and things have been a little crazy around here."

"I'm not calling about the seminar, Grace. I'm calling to find out if you're interested in meeting someone."

It took a few moments for Grace to recover from her surprise.

Meredith Boothe had done the home study for the adoption agency Grace was working with, but their careers and personalities had blended so well that they'd become good friends over the past few months, spending time together both professionally and socially.

"I don't think so," she said politely, wondering how she could decline without hurting Meredith's feelings. "I'm sure he's a nice guy and everything, but…" Grace didn't know quite what to say but it didn't matter.

A burst of laughter on the other end of the line finished her sentence. "Not a date!"

"Oh." Grace would have felt silly for jumping to conclusions if she hadn't been so relieved.

"Yesterday, one of the couples I've been working with changed their mind about adoption," Meredith continued. "And that means a little boy named Michael needs a home."

Grace's knees turned to liquid and she slid into the closest chair. "But…you said it could take months." *Years.*

"Well, God's timing isn't always the same as ours." There was a short pause as Meredith let the news sink in. "But that said, you don't have to make a decision right at this moment," she added gently. "Take some time to pray about it. You and I can sit down and talk. You can meet Michael and—"

"Yes."

Meredith chuckled. "Yes to which part?"

Grace swiped at a tear rolling down her cheek.

"All of it."

Chapter Fifteen

"Do you have a minute?"

Cole took one look at Matt Wilde's expression and fig-ured whatever the pastor wanted to say to him was going to take more time than that. He nodded anyway.

"Sure."

Matt smiled. "Great. I'll meet you by the dock in five minutes."

Great.

If Cole's suspicions proved correct, this would be his sec-ond serious conversation of the morning. The first one had taken place ten minutes before he'd left for church.

His mom had called when the ship docked for a few hours to give him an update about a change in the cruise itinerary. To say she'd been shocked to discover he was in Mirror Lake was an understatement.

Cole hadn't planned on telling his mother about Sloan's will until she and George returned from their honeymoon, but somehow she'd managed to finagle all the details. Then she'd given the phone to George so Cole could repeat them.

Which was the reason he'd been late for church.

At least seventy-five people had gathered for the outdoor worship service, making it difficult to spot Grace in the crowd. Everyone's attention was focused on the two women playing a violin duet, so Cole had slipped into one of the empty wooden benches in the back row.

He closed his eyes and tried to let the melody of the worship song sand away the edges of his restless thoughts.

"Can I sit here?"

The words were so quiet, Cole thought he'd imagined them. But when he turned around, Cody Lang was standing behind him.

Cole had slid down to make room. "Have you seen Grace?"

"Zoey needed her help with the little kids," Cody had said in a low whisper. "They have a special service in the garden."

Cole had felt the knot in his stomach unravel a bit.

He wasn't sure why the thought of seeing her again made him nervous.

Maybe because you kissed her?

Yeah, there was that.

But he hadn't been toying with her emotions. He'd meant what he said. He wanted to get to know her again.

Living so far apart would pose a challenge, but other couples managed to make it work. They could talk on the phone. He could drive up on the weekends....

Cody had nudged his elbow. "We're supposed to stand up for this part."

Flushing slightly, Cole followed the boy's lead and rose to his feet to join Pastor Matt and the rest of the congregation in prayer.

Matt's message had dovetailed with the mayor's speech the day before about fellowship. Working together. Bearing each other's burdens.

Cole hadn't been very good at the last one. Oh, he'd done everything he could to ease the load on his mother's shoulders, to make his siblings' lives easier, but it occurred to Cole that he hadn't let anyone help him. At least not until Lily had barged into their lives.

It was one of the things that had kept Cole awake during the night. Grace had seemed hurt, not appreciative, that he hadn't confided in her twelve years ago.

Cole had never thought of it from her perspective. Until Matt had read the verse from Ecclesiastes he'd heard Grace share with Haylie the day before.

Two are better than one, for they have a good return for their work.

It made Cole uncomfortably aware that at least in one respect, he had taken after his grandfather. No matter how tough things were, he'd never reached out and asked for help.

"Abby made me promise I'd say a blessing over the food but we have some time while they're setting up the refreshments."

Cole had been so lost in thought he hadn't heard the pastor approach.

"I'm glad you decided to join us this morning." Matt started down the shoreline and Cole automatically fell in step with him.

"The outdoor service was a great idea."

"I'll tell Zoey." Matt grinned. "To be honest, my wife comes up with ninety-nine percent of the great ideas. God knew exactly what I needed and He brought her into my life at just the right time. I'm not sure what she gets out of it, though."

Cole smiled because he knew it was expected of him. The pastor seemed like a regular kind of guy, down-to-earth and easy to talk to. He just wasn't sure what Matt wanted to talk *about*.

Had he seen him with Grace at the fireworks?

Oh, who was he kidding?

Everyone had seen them together at the fireworks. And he'd kissed her…in front of everyone.

If the pastor was as protective of Grace as the rest of her friends were, Cole figured he was about to receive another lecture.

Matt slanted a look at him. "You're probably wondering what this is about."

"Grace?"

"Actually, no." Matt's lips quirked. "But now that you brought it up, maybe I should add her name to the agenda."

Cole knew he had had no one to blame but himself for opening that door.

"Let's sit for a minute." Matt angled his head toward a freestanding wooden swing near the rustic cabins scattered along the shoreline. Far enough from the bed-and-breakfast, Cole noticed, so no one would overhear their conversation.

The pastor sat down and stretched his legs out in front of him but didn't comment on the fact that Cole chose to remain standing.

"Sloan told me about his will."

It was the last thing Cole had expected Matt to say.

"Why?" he asked bluntly.

Matt hesitated, searching Cole's face with the same intensity he appeared to be searching for the right words.

"Sometimes, when a man gets to the end of his life, he begins to think about the years he's lived rather than the ones he has left. Sloan admitted that he'd made a lot of mistakes."

"Mistakes don't always equal regrets." Cole's back teeth ground together so he wouldn't say something *he* would regret.

"That's true. But in your grandfather's case, I believe they did."

"He regretted the way he treated my parents?"

"And you."

"Me?" Cole practically choked on the word.

"Sloan talked about you a lot."

"He didn't even know me." Cole winced when he heard the bitterness leach into his voice. He thought he'd forgiven his grandfather. Put the past behind him. "In fact, I have no clue why he left his entire estate to me. Why not give it to my mom? Or split it equally between me and my brothers and sister?"

"You've been wondering if it was a deliberate attempt to cause trouble? To divide your family?"

Cole was taken aback by Matt's insight. And honesty. It challenged him to respond in kind.

"I wouldn't put it past him."

"There were things Sloan said that should remain in confidence, even now that he's gone," Matt said slowly. "But under the circumstances, I think you should know why he set up his will the way he did."

"He *told* you?"

Matt nodded. "The last time we spoke."

Cole's hands fisted at his sides. He'd tried to convince himself it didn't matter why his grandfather had left the house and land to him; the only thing he cared about was how much it was worth.

"You know that piece of property has been in your family since the town was settled."

"Yes." Thanks to Grace, he'd overheard an abbreviated version of his family history.

"From what I've heard, Samuel Merrick had a strong faith and a strong commitment to family. He passed that on to his son, Cade."

"Well, somehow it skipped a few generations. Sloan disowned my dad when he was eighteen just because he married my mom." A muscle worked in Cole's jaw. "He told him to leave. After Dad died, he told us to leave, too."

"You may not believe me, but Sloan regretted that the most." A shadow passed through Matt's eyes. "He didn't know how to make things right."

"A phone call would have worked."

"I tried to encourage him to contact your family, but he was afraid."

"Of being rejected?" The irony wasn't lost on Cole. "I wrote him a letter, telling him that I'd forgiven him."

"Sloan mentioned that. I'm just not sure he ever forgave himself. With the choices he'd made during his life, your grandfather's memories didn't bring any comfort as his health began to decline. He said he didn't want your memory of him to be the one where he stood on the porch and told you to leave."

"He did the same thing to my dad."

"Sloan couldn't forget that, either. He wanted to make it up to you."

"By not letting anyone contact me about the will?" Cole shook his head.

"He said he wanted to leave this in God's hands. He believed you would find out about the property at the right time."

"I did, but that was God's doing, not my grandfather's. The money I make from the sale is going into the business I own."

Matt smiled.

"What?"

"A verse from Proverbs just came to mind, that's all. *'In his heart a man plans his course, but the Lord determines his steps.'* Sometimes God has another plan. One we don't see right away."

"There are more reasons to sell than there are to hold on to it."

"All I know is that Sloan wanted you to have the property," Matt said evenly. "He said it's part of your legacy."

"Part of my legacy." Cole knew he sounded defensive, but he was getting a little tired of that word. "What's the rest of it?"

Matt clapped a hand on his shoulder.

"That's up to you."

"He's with Matt." Emma breezed past with a tray of fresh fruit. "Just in case you were wondering."

"I wasn't wondering…much," Grace muttered.

"Uh-huh." Laughter kindled in Emma's blue-gray eyes. "You two looked pretty cozy at the fireworks last night."

"I think they *started* the fireworks last night." Kate had entered the kitchen.

"I'm not having this conversation!" Grace howled.

"That's all right." Kate gave Grace's shoulder a quick pat. "We'll have it for you."

"I'm taking the vegetable tray outside now."

"We're going to set up the buffet table on the deck," Abby said. "Quinn mentioned there's a thunderstorm moving in later this afternoon, and we might have to move everything inside."

"I'm glad it didn't rain yesterday." Emma snitched a piece of watermelon from the tray. "Jake and I never would have gotten that fire started."

"You *didn't* get your fire started," Kate teased.

Grace decided there would never be a better time to sneak outside. She hadn't had an opportunity to talk to Cole, but she'd spotted him walking toward the benches lined up under the canopy of willow trees shortly after the service had started. He had made room for Cody, which had only triggered that funny little catch in her heart again.

The time they'd been apart had shaped Cole's character in ways Grace hadn't expected. He was more patient. More responsible than he'd been at seventeen.

It gave her courage to tell him about the phone call she'd received after she'd gotten home the night before.

Grace might have dismissed the entire evening as a dream if she'd been able to fall asleep.

Meredith had insisted they meet to discuss the details in person, so she didn't know anything more than what her friend had shared on the phone. Grace had checked her calendar and set up a time to meet after work on Tuesday.

She slipped outside and was immediately surrounded by the first graders who attended her Sunday school class.

"Miss Grace! Can you go for a walk with us? Pleeease?" Molly, one of the most adorable little girls Grace had ever taught, had been appointed the official spokesperson for the group. "Tori's dad showed her a nest with two baby eagles in it, and their mama feeds them *fish*."

"Is that right?" Grace knelt down so she was eye to eye with Tori. Molly and Jenna's niece had become inseparable over the course of the school year, another encouraging sign she'd settled into her new life. "And where do these baby eagles live?"

"They're at the top of the crooked tree." The girl's periwinkle blue eyes sparkled with excitement. "We can watch the mama feed her babies if we don't disturb them."

Grace didn't have to ask where the tree was located. In a town surrounded by thousands of acres of national forest, everyone in Mirror Lake knew the "crooked tree." The hundred-year-old white pine, sprouting from a narrow peninsula not far from the stone chapel on Abby's property, was practically a local landmark.

"My mom said I can go, too," Brody chimed in. "If you're with us. And if I eat one bite of broccoli."

Sunday school classes had dismissed for the summer several weeks ago, and Grace already missed the children. A hike would give her an opportunity to spend some time with them.

"I'd love to go. We can leave right after lunch." She winked at Brody. "Broccoli first."

The children squealed as they ran off to tell their parents.

Grace set the fruit tray down on the buffet table and spotted Matt walking up the hill. Alone. She intercepted him before someone else did.

"Hi, Pastor."

"Grace." Matt's warm smile had a way of lifting a person's spirits. "Thank you for volunteering to help Zoey with children's church at the last minute."

"It's always fun to work with Zoey. She's great with the preschoolers."

"So are you."

"Do you really think so?" The words slipped out before she could stop them.

"You're kidding, right? The kids love you." Matt's eyes narrowed when she didn't respond. "You don't look too sure."

At the moment, Grace wasn't sure about a lot of things.

She'd wanted to talk to Matt about Meredith's phone call, but decided now wasn't the best time to bring it up. The pastor deserved a day off, too.

"Will you pray for me this week?" Grace had to ask before lost her courage. "I have a...decision to make."

"There seems to be a lot of that going around." Matt glanced over his shoulder.

Grace followed his gaze and saw Cole sitting on a weathered cedar swing near the cabins.

A crazy thought suddenly occurred to her.

"You aren't matchmaking, are you?"

"Grace Eversea." Matt's eyebrows shot up. "I can't believe you even have to ask that."

"Sorry," Grace murmured.

"Apology accepted, because I'm probably the only one in this town who doesn't matchmake." A hint of laughter danced in his hazel eyes. "My job is to encourage fellowship."

Chapter Sixteen

"Mom just told me."

Cole tried not to cringe when he heard his sister's lilting voice over the phone. And here he thought news traveled fast in a small town.

"How is Scotland?"

"Oh, no, you don't! Right now, what's happening in Mirror Lake is way more interesting than Edinburgh."

Cole had to agree, but he wasn't about to tell his baby sister that.

"I can't believe Mom called you." *From the cruise ship. In Alaska.*

"And I can't believe *you* didn't," Bettina retorted. "This is big news, Cole."

"What exactly did Mom say?"

"To ask you if I wanted information. So, I'm asking!"

"A few days ago, I found out Sloan left the house and land to me when he died. I drove up here to talk to his attorney."

Absolute silence followed. Because his nineteen-year-old sister was never at a loss for words, Cole figured they'd been disconnected. Until he heard a gurgle on the other end of the line.

"Bets?"

"That is…" His sister paused.

Unbelievable? *Unfair?* Cole silently filled in the blank. It wouldn't be the first time he felt a stab of guilt that his siblings hadn't been mentioned in their grandfather's will.

"Great."

"Great?" Cole echoed.

"I've thought about that place a lot over the years," she said after a moment, stunning him into silence.

"You have?"

"There was an old root cellar behind the house that I turned into a playhouse. I smuggled some dishes from the kitchen and hosted tea parties for my stuffed animals."

"I didn't know that."

"Well, you *were* kind of…preoccupied. Putting your faith into action."

"My faith?"

Bettina giggled. "Love thy neighbor?"

Cole felt his face grow warm. He couldn't even blame the sun, which had disappeared behind a bank of gray clouds.

"I—" he choked out, ready to deny it.

"Don't bother trying to deny it, either. The boys and I hid in the bushes and spied on you."

"Brat." The nickname had become an endearment over the years.

"I liked Grandpa Sloan's place." Bettina's tone sounded wistful. "It was peaceful."

Peaceful wouldn't have been the word Cole would have chosen. Not with the tension that existed, as thick as the pockets of evening mist that settled between the trees, between their mother and Sloan.

"It's gotten pretty run-down over the past few years."

"Then we can fix it up."

"Fix it?" Cole frowned. "Hold on a sec—"

"I mean, the hangar is great, but you have to admit it's

small," she chatted on. "There isn't much privacy, not with people coming and going all the time."

"I'm planning to sell it," Cole said flatly. "That's one of the reasons why I'm here."

"Why would you do that?" Bettina sounded as shocked by the news he wanted to sell the property as he was that she'd actually thought he would want to keep it.

"Why?" Because he needed the money to expand his business. Time to focus on Painted Skies. "It's too far away. The upkeep wouldn't be easy. And—" he couldn't help but point this out "—you're in college nine months out of the year and the twins are going to be stationed who knows where after basic training. When would you have time to visit?"

"Maybe we wouldn't at first. But when the boys and I get married and start having kids, it will be nice to have a place where we can meet on vacation."

Did his baby sister just use the words *marriage* and *kids* in the same sentence?

Because Cole's brothers considered a slice of pizza, a can of Mountain Dew and a Snickers bar a three-course meal. Bettina hadn't been able to part with her collection of stuffed animals when she'd left for college. She'd packed them all up and taken them along.

And she *lost* important pieces of mail.

Not knowing how to recite the evidence without offending his sister, Cole retreated into humor.

"You're not old enough to get married."

"You aren't anxious to be the favorite uncle?" Bettina teased.

"Mmm, let me think about that. Wiping noses. Bandaging wounds. Watching Disney movies instead of Monday night football." Cole paused. *"No."*

"You'll change your mind. You have to. Who else am I

supposed to leave the children with while my husband and I go to Hawaii on our anniversary?"

Bettina wasn't even engaged and already she was talking about celebrating her anniversary?

"My days of raising children are over. I served my time."

"But look what a great job you did with us." His sister's voice had softened, weighted with meaning. With memories.

"That's debatable."

Feminine laughter erupted in the background. "My roommates are back now, so I better go. It was good to talk to you, Cole. I miss you."

"You, too." He pushed the words through the lump that had formed in his throat.

"And Cole? It's okay if you sell grandpa's land. I understand. You've done so much for all of us…it's time to do something for yourself."

Then why, Cole thought as he slipped the phone back in his pocket, didn't it *feel* okay?

My days of raising children are over.

Grace's hands curled at her sides, almost crushing the stems of the dandelion bouquet one of the preschool girls had picked for her.

Everything Cole had told her about his family suddenly took on a whole new meaning. One Grace hadn't considered until this moment.

While his friends had gone off to college or found full-time jobs, Cole had stayed at home, caring for his family while struggling to make ends meet.

There hadn't been a trace of resentment in his eyes. No hint of bitterness. But he *had* sounded excited about the fact that his siblings were independent now; his mother remarried to a man who loved and accepted her.

No wonder Cole wanted to sell the property. It would bring him one step closer to realizing his dreams.

Somehow, over the past forty-eight hours, Grace had lost sight of the truth. She'd been distracted by Cole's smile.

His kiss.

She'd been ready to give her heart to him all over again if, Grace acknowledged with a painful burst of clarity, it hadn't been in his keeping for the past twelve years.

Her friends had teased her on occasion, asking what was wrong with the men who asked her out. Grace had never been able to answer. But maybe, just maybe, they'd simply made the mistake of not being…Cole.

I served my time.

Meaning he was free now.

Cole's tone might have been lighthearted, but the underlying message had been clear: He had no desire to be tied down.

Grace had dreamed of having a family for years. Prayed about adopting a baby for months before she'd contacted the agency.

Trusted God's timing.

I don't understand, Lord. Why now?

She took a cautious step back, poised to escape before Cole realized she was there. The movement must have caught his attention because he twisted around.

"Grace." His eyes lit up when he saw her, a response that would have given Grace hope. If she hadn't overheard his conversation.

"Hi."

Cole rose to his feet with a smile that made Grace's heart buckle. She couldn't think straight when Cole looked at her that way. "I must have missed the dinner bell."

She glanced over her shoulder and saw people carrying their plates to the picnic tables set up on the lawn.

"I think Abby is worried it's going to rain," Grace murmured.

"I guess we better get in line, then." Cole reached for her hand, but Grace quickened her pace, safely out of his reach for the moment.

"I'm not very hungry...I should probably help Abby and Kate in the kitchen."

"I can save you a seat—"

"I've already got one with your name on it!"

Grace had never been so relieved to see Sissy Perkins in her life.

The Realtor linked arms with Cole. "I met someone a few minutes ago who wants to talk to you about a certain piece of property."

"I'm not sure this a good time."

"Honey, it's *always* a good time to talk about property." Sissy's enthusiasm wasn't dampened by Cole's frown. "Especially when there are no contingencies and the buyer has been preapproved."

"You should talk to them." Grace pinned on a smile. "It's what you wanted, right?"

Sissy whisked Cole away before he had a chance to respond, but it didn't matter.

She knew what Cole wanted. And now, because she'd eavesdropped on a private conversation, she knew what he didn't.

My days of raising children are over.

After the sacrifices he'd made, Grace knew it wasn't fair to expect him to put his dreams on hold again.

But she wasn't sure if she could give up hers, either.

Cole smiled as he watched the children fall into line behind Grace like a row of ducklings as they made their way down the path.

He'd finally managed to excuse himself from the table, where Sissy and a heart surgeon from Chicago had discussed everything but his asking price, only to discover that Grace had offered to take Tori Gardner and three other children on a short hike.

Cole was anxious to talk to her, but with all the curious eyes that had been fixed on them, he knew it would be better to wait until they were alone.

Something he was beginning to doubt would happen anytime soon.

"There it is!" Brody had stopped in the middle of the trail. He pointed at a white pine growing on the tip of a narrow peninsula that jutted over the water. Cradled in the top of the branches was a very large nest that could have only been created by a very large bird.

"Shh." Molly scowled at her friend. "The babies might be sleeping."

He tried to catch Grace's eye, but she wouldn't look at him. Come to think of it, she hadn't looked at him for quite a while.

Cole tried to ignore the unease that sluiced through his veins and left him feeling chilled.

Things were moving a little fast between them, but in some ways, it seemed as if they'd never been apart. After last night, Cole was sure Grace felt the same way.

"Why don't we sit over there and watch for a bit?" Grace suggested. "Maybe the mother eagle will come back."

Four small heads bobbed in unison.

They chose a spot close enough to see the eaglets, but far enough away so their mother wouldn't be upset when she returned.

Grace sat down in a grassy area and wrapped her arms around the girls while Brody and his sidekick, Riley, settled near her feet.

"You can sit down, too." Tori smiled up at him. "There's room by Miss Grace."

Cole wasn't going to turn down the invitation.

As the minutes ticked by, Grace listened patiently while the boys tried to outdo each other with stories about their last fishing trip. She traded bracelets with Tori—swapping the thin gold chain around her wrist for a strand of sparkly pink beads—and sat perfectly still while Molly braided a daisy in her hair.

Cole was more enchanted by the sound of Grace's laughter than he was by the beauty of their surroundings.

Forty-eight hours ago, he couldn't wait to take care of business and leave Mirror Lake for good. Now he wished he could stay a few more days.

"Look!" Grace pointed to the sky. "There she is."

All four children lapsed into silence as they watched the mother eagle circled the tree a few times and then land in the nest, a fish clamped in her hooked beak.

Cole wasn't sure how long they stayed there listening to the eaglets squabble over their portions, but the boys started to fidget when the mother eagle finally settled into the nest with her family.

"Can we explore a little, Miss Grace?" Riley pleaded. "Jeremy and Cody found an arrowhead last week, and we want to find one, too."

Grace smiled. "Ten more minutes."

The high-pitched squeals of excitement that followed made Cole wince. "And I thought those baby eagles made a lot of noise."

"You don't have to stick around." Grace started after the boys. "I know you have a lot to do before you go home."

"But I'm coming back next weekend." Cole reached for her hand. "We have a date, remember?"

Grace didn't pull her hand away. But she didn't answer,

proof that his suspicions had been correct. Something *was* wrong. What was at the root of her uncertainty? His feelings? Or hers?

"Do you have another tour scheduled?"

"I have one before the closing ceremony tonight. Why?"

"I'd like to go along. I think it's time I learned about the Merrick family."

Cole had hoped that would bring a smile to her face. He wasn't prepared to see her eyes mist over.

"I better check on the kids." She moved away from him, working her way between the trees.

"Grace?" It didn't take Cole more than a second to catch up to her, but the expression on her face made it feel as if they were miles apart. "What's going on?"

"Nothing…really. Everything is fine."

"Then why won't you look at me?"

Instead of answering, Grace vaulted over a fallen tree. "It looks like the sky is getting dark."

A split second later, a low growl of thunder backed up the words.

Tori raced up to them and attached herself to Grace's leg.

"I don't like that noise," she whimpered.

"I'll be right back." Cole worked his way through the trees and stepped back onto the trail.

What he saw bearing down on them chilled his blood. On the other side of the lake, a dark haze fell from a swirling mass of clouds like a curtain, its ragged hem sweeping the surface of the water. Making it difficult to see where one ended and the other began.

He motioned to Grace. "It's time to head back."

Cole had tried to keep his voice from betraying his concern, but Grace was at his side in an instant, her eyes wide with alarm when she saw the sky.

"Come on, everyone. It looks like the storm we're supposed to get this afternoon decided to show up early. We'll have to hurry so we can get to the inn before it does."

Judging from the speed of the clouds bearing down on the lake, Cole has his doubts that would happen.

"The sky is a funny color," Molly announced.

Unfortunately, Cole had to agree. He'd only seen that eerie shade of green once before, when a funnel cloud had dropped from the sky and shaved a path a half mile wide through a nearby cornfield.

He looked at Grace. "We're not going to make it back before the storm hits."

"The chapel isn't too far away." She had to pitch her voice above the high-pitched keening of the wind. "Should we go there?"

"I don't think we have much of a choice."

Trees began to bow as they struggled up the path. Grace stretched her arms over the children, trying to shield them against the drops of rain that pelted the ground.

Brody cupped his hands around Cole's ear. "I hear fire trucks!"

Cole's gaze snagged with Grace's over the boy's head and even before he saw the flash of fear in her eyes, he recognized the sound.

Not fire trucks.

A siren.

Warning everyone in the area to seek shelter.

Chapter Seventeen

"I'm scared!"

"I know, sweetie. Stay close to me." Grace wrapped her arm around Tori's thin shoulders. "Do you remember the stone chapel? We're going to stay there until it stops raining, and then Cole and I will take you to your parents, okay?"

"Okay." The little girl pressed closer to her side.

Cole flashed Grace a reassuring smile that didn't extinguish the concern banked in his eyes. "Lead the way."

She tried to calculate the quickest way to reach the chapel. It was dangerous to be in the woods during a thunderstorm, but doubling back and following the trail would take more time.

Her heart jumped in time with the muffled thud of a tree hitting the ground not far away.

God, protect us.

"This way." Grace surged forward, battling not only the wind, but the guilt that came from knowing she'd put the children in danger by not paying close enough attention to the weather.

Cole was a step behind her, his very presence keeping her own fears at bay. When she stumbled, it was his hand that shot out and steadied her.

Tori's shoulders began to shake with silent sobs, and Grace pulled her closer. Kate had mentioned the little girl was terrified of storms and the dark, and now they had to contend with both. It was only three o'clock, but the thick clouds boiling over their heads formed an impenetrable barrier, blocking out the afternoon sun.

Just when Grace was beginning to worry she was leading Cole and the children in the wrong direction, the wind shifted and she spotted a small stone structure through the veil of rain. She sent up a silent prayer that Abby and Quinn had left the door of the chapel unlocked.

The same thought must have run through Cole's mind because he sprinted ahead of them. Grace held her breath as he wrestled it open.

"It's dark in there." Tori balked on the step as Grace tried to urge her and Molly inside.

"I've got you." Cole swept Tori up in his arms and kicked the door shut. The sound ricocheted against the walls.

"There's a small room in the back." Grace took Tori and Molly by the hand and guided them between the wooden pews.

She discovered a bundle of clean rags stashed in a small cupboard and used them to mop up the expanding puddles of water that dripped from the children's hair and clothing.

Hail began to ping against the roof like shotgun pellets and all four children started to cry.

"I wanna go home!" Riley howled.

Grace knelt down and blotted the rain from his pudgy cheeks. "We'll be okay, sweetheart."

"How do you…know?" Molly sniffled.

"Because we're in church," Brody piped up. "And that means Jesus is here, right, Miss Grace?"

Cole laughed. The sound was so unexpected, the children turned to stare at him.

So did Grace.

"He's not just in church, buddy. He's everywhere." Cole ruffled the spikes of wet hair that sprouted from Brody's head. "Didn't Grace tell you the story about the time Jesus and his friends were caught in a bad storm?"

"Not yet," Molly said. "But she tells us lots of stories."

"I guess that means I'll have to tell this one." Cole dropped to the floor and settled his back against the wall. Immediately all four children crowded into his lap. "Jesus and his friends were in a boat on the lake, not a cozy little building like this one. Waves crashed over the side and there was thunder and lightning."

A shudder ripped through Tori's tiny frame. "Was Jesus scared, too?"

"Nope. He was sound asleep. In fact, his friends had to wake him up." Cole stretched out his legs, as if they were gathered in a comfortable living room instead of an oversize closet while a storm raged just beyond the wall. "Do you know what he told them?"

Tori sniffled. "W-what?"

"He told them not to be afraid. He was right there with them in that boat and he's with us, too. He knows how we feel and we can ask him anytime to help us not to be afraid."

"Can we ask Him now?" Molly asked in a small voice.

Cole smiled. "We sure can."

Grace closed her eyes, holding back the tears that threatened to spill over as Cole began to pray.

"You know we're here, Lord. You know we're a little afraid of the wind and all the racket out there. But You promise that You are with us even in the middle of a storm and we trust You to take care of us—"

"Amen!" Riley's exuberant benediction momentarily drowned out the sound of the rain.

Grace released a ragged breath. She should have recognized the source of the changes she'd seen in Cole. Time hadn't sanded down the rough edges. Neither had the responsibility of caring for his family. His *faith* had.

Grace slid a glance at Cole, only to find him watching her. He nodded, as if she'd asked him a question.

Even while they'd been apart, God had continued to work in Cole's life. Grace had encouraged him to turn to God for strength that summer, never knowing he had taken her advice to heart.

If that was the reason He had brought them together, Grace decided it had been worth the pain of letting Cole go.

Minutes seemed like hours as they waited for the rattle of the wind to subside.

"I think the storm moved past." Cole gently dislodged the children from his lap and pushed to his feet. "I'll be right back."

The children wanted to follow, but Grace had them wait by the door until Cole indicated it was safe to go outdoors. When he waved to Grace from the doorway, they scrambled past her.

Grace's knees buckled when she stepped outside the chapel and saw the damage.

The wind had stripped the trees of their leaves, leaving them strewn on the ground like confetti. One of the stately pines had been snapped off at the base and a grove of poplar trees had been uprooted, leaving gaping holes in the ground. Hail the size of glass beads littered the grass.

"It snowed!" Brody scooped a handful of icy pellets off the ground.

She moved to Cole's side. "Tornado?" she murmured in a low voice so the children wouldn't hear their conversation.

"From what I can see, there doesn't seem to be a pattern with the damage."

From what he could see. But what about they *couldn't* see?

"Do you think—" Grace didn't finish the thought. "We have to get back. Their parents are going to be worried sick."

Grace and Cole held the children's hands while they picked their way down the muddy path, dodging puddles and fallen branches.

People were streaming out of the inn when they emerged from the woods a few minutes later. Grace heard a startled cry and saw Jenna running toward them. Dev and Logan were only a few steps behind.

"I'm sorry," Grace gasped as Dev picked up Tori. "The storm came in so fast…we went to the chapel."

"Don't apologize." Jenna squeezed her arm. "None of us had a lot of time to prepare. One minute we were putting away the lawn chairs and the next minute we were chasing them across the yard."

In less than five minutes, the rest of the children had been reunited with their parents.

Abby dashed up to her. "Are you all right?"

"I was just about to ask you the same thing." Grace hugged her friend.

"Everyone is fine. Here."

"What do you mean?"

"Jake got a call from a county officer a few minutes ago. A tornado touched down a few miles north of town, on Timber Drive." Abby bit her lip. "He's on his way over there right now."

Timber Drive.

Grace tried to remember how many houses were located along the road and her mouth went dry.

"The campground?"

Abby nodded. "According to Officer West, it would have been right in its path. Jake isn't sure if the people staying there even had time to make it to safety."

Grace's stomach clenched. The small campground didn't have a pavilion or shelter of any kind. Most of the campers set up tents rather than expensive motor homes.

"Did Quinn go with him?"

"He and Alex went with Matt to move a tree that's blocking one of the roads or I would have sent them along to help."

"I'll go. I'm volunteer with the local rescue squad." Cole turned to Grace. "Can you tell me how to get to the campground?"

"I can show you."

"Is it gonna sting?"

Adam, the five-year-old boy one of the officers had discovered hiding under the twisted remains of a pop-up camper, scooted away from Cole as he removed a bottle of antiseptic from the first aid kit.

"A little," Cole said truthfully. "Can you count to five?"

"Uh-huh."

"Great. Start counting and I promise by the time you get to five, it won't hurt anymore."

Adam's lower lip quivered. "Okay."

"Good boy." Cole opened another package and removed a gauze bandage. Considering the amount of damage the tornado had caused, the boy was lucky he'd only suffered a few minor cuts and scrapes.

Adam's grandfather hadn't been quite as fortunate. The EMTs who had been called to the scene were getting ready to transport him to a local hospital.

"How are you doing, champ?" Jake Sutton plunked his navy blue police cap on Adam's head and was rewarded with a soft giggle.

Cole had met the police chief briefly the day before, when Jake and Emma had pitched in to raise the shelter for the competition.

By the time he and Grace had arrived, Jake and a local game warden had taken charge of the scene, sending volunteers to check the campsites. Cole began to treat the injured campers who'd taken shelter in a metal utility shed and Grace had offered to help one of the female officers check the list of campers to make sure everyone was accounted for.

"There's a guy over there with a lump on his head the size of a tennis ball," Jake said in a low voice. "He says he's fine, but can you take a look at it?"

"No problem."

Adam began to fidget. "Where's my gramma? I wanna see her."

"You're all done, champ." Cole closed up the first aid kit. "And I'm sure your grandma is anxious to see you, too."

"I'll take him over there." Jake picked up the boy and carried him over to the ambulance, where his grandmother was talking with the paramedic who'd treated her husband.

Cole grabbed an ice pack and made his way over to the young man slumped over on the tailgate of a pickup. He spent the next ten minutes trying to convince the guy that yes, he had suffered a minor concussion and needed medical attention.

On his way back to confer with the rescue workers, he spotted the female officer Grace had left with.

"Hey." Cole changed course and jogged over to her. "Where is Grace?"

The officer frowned. "She's not back yet?"

"Back from where? Wasn't she helping you?"

"One of the campers mentioned there was a couple staying in one of the rustic cabins. There's three of them, about a mile up the road."

"I thought Jake said everyone was accounted for."

"Everyone who *registered*. Sometimes people notice the

cabins are empty and they decide to stay there without paying the fee."

"Who went with her?" Sutton had materialized at Cole's side.

Although the inflection in Jake's voice didn't change, some of the color drained from the woman's face.

"She said I should stay here to help…she didn't mind going alone."

Alone.

The word continued to cycle through Cole's mind as the tires of his SUV chewed through the branches that littered the dirt road. Some of them were the size of small trees. Cole inched the car around, between and over them.

About three quarters of a mile, Jake had said.

Which meant he had to be getting close.

A whitetail deer leaped out of the ditch and landed in front of the car. Cole stomped on the brake to avoid hitting it.

The headlights illuminated the red pine lying across the road less than ten yards away. Grace's truck was parked at an angle in front of it.

There was no one inside.

He tipped his head back and slammed his hands against the steering wheel.

Okay, God. Now what?

He hopped out of the car and strode over to the tree to see if he could get around it. It was half the tree, the other part was a few feet from the ditch, sticking out of the ground like a broken matchstick, the jagged splinters charred from the lightning that had sliced it in two.

Cole turned slowly, considering the list of options that were swiftly dwindling down to two. He could either turn around and find another way to the cabins. Or he could do what Grace had done. Go the rest of the way on foot.

A breeze rattled the trees, and Cole got an instant shower from the moisture that glazed the leaves above his head. He grabbed the nylon jacket from the trunk of his SUV and shrugged it on.

Three cabins, none of them with electricity or running water, according to the warden.

Grace was smart, Cole reminded himself. If she'd run into trouble, she'd find a way to let someone know where she was. He stuck to the road until he saw the boxy silhouette of a cabin in the distance.

And a light flickering in the window.

Thank You, Lord.

As he reached the front door, a shrill cry pierced the air.

Cole didn't bother to knock. He burst inside and felt his heart turn over in his chest.

Two figures—one young woman lying prone on a narrow bunk bed attached to the wall—the other...

"*Grace.*"

A pair of chocolate-brown eyes locked on his face. Grace, who'd been kneeling by the bunk, pushed to her feet and took one wobbly step toward him.

Cole caught her against him on the second.

"How did you..." The sentence chipped off. "This is Stephanie. She needs some help."

A low moan from the woman on the bed backed up Grace's statement. She broke away from Cole and hurried back to the younger woman's side.

"What happened?" Cole's mind shifted into high gear, working out the logistics of how to get an injured girl back to the campground as he strode toward the bunk. "Where is she hurt?"

Grace reached for the girl's hand.

"Stephanie isn't injured. She's in labor."

Chapter Eighteen

All Grace wanted to do was wrap her arms around Cole and lean against his solid chest. To feel the steady beat of his heart against hers and know he wasn't a figment of her imagination.

The last hour had become a blur. When she'd discovered Stephanie, the eighteen-year-old had been writhing on the cot and hugging a tattered sleeping bag against her swollen abdomen, crying out for someone named Bryce.

Grace had almost turned the car around when she'd seen the tree down in the road, but something had prompted her to go into the woods on foot and check the cabin. She'd found Stephanie alone and in labor and was thankful she'd listened to what she now realized had been a divine nudge.

The terrified girl had begged her not to leave, so Grace had held her hand through the next contraction and silently asked God to send someone to help them.

She just hadn't expected it to be Cole.

"How far apart are the contractions?" He knelt down beside the cot and pressed his fingers against Stephanie's wrist.

"Seven minutes."

"Okay." Cole's jaw tightened, the only outward sign that he'd been hoping for another response.

"Who are you?" Stephanie's wild-eyed gaze bounced back and forth between them. "Did Bryce send you? Is he all right?"

"Bryce is Stephanie's boyfriend," Grace explained.

The guy who had left her alone after they'd argued the day before. If it hadn't been for the hiker who'd mentioned he had heard voices inside the cabin the day before, Grace doubted anyone would have known the couple was staying there.

"I haven't met Bryce, but I'm sure he's fine." Cole's voice was soothing, his movements gentle and unhurried as he lifted Stephanie into a sitting position. "My name is Cole and I'm trained as an EMT."

"It…hurts." Tears filled Stephanie's eyes. "I'm not due for three weeks."

Cole smiled. "Babies sometimes have their own agenda, but I promise we'll get you to the hospital as soon as we can."

Stephanie doubled over with a harsh gasp, and Grace reached for her hand, murmuring words of encouragement.

"Cell phone?" Cole murmured.

Grace shook her head. "No reception."

"I guess that explains why you didn't return my calls." He shot her a teasing look and then sobered. "I'll need you to round up a sheet or some clean towels."

Grace didn't need to ask why. Cole wanted to be prepared if he had to deliver the baby.

"All right." She tried to match her tone to his, calm and steady.

She could hear Cole talking to Stephanie as she searched for the items he'd requested. The rustic, one-room cabin didn't offer much in the way of amenities, but Grace found a terrycloth beach towel among Stephanie's things.

"This is all I could find." She held it up for Cole's inspection.

"Perfect." Cole smiled, but the shadow of concern in his

eyes warned Grace that something else was wrong. "I offered to get in touch with Stephanie's doctor and have him meet us at the hospital, but she hasn't been to see one yet."

Grace expelled a silent breath, heartbroken but not surprised. She'd counseled several teenaged girls over the years who'd been too embarrassed or ashamed to ask for help and tried to keep their pregnancy a secret.

But no doctor meant no prenatal care. No ultrasounds. If the baby did arrive before they reached the hospital, there'd be no way of knowing if there was a condition that might put the mother and baby at risk.

"Hey." Cole squeezed her hand. "Two are better than one, remember? We'll get Stephanie back to the campground and call for an ambulance."

"I like that plan," the girl croaked.

"Then let's go." Cole drew Stephanie to her feet. As they slowly made their way outside, he became the anchor holding the girl in place as another contraction left her weak and trembling.

He glanced at Grace, and she held up five fingers.

Cole tipped his head toward the sky, a silent reminder to pray. Something she hadn't stopped doing since the storm had rolled through.

"Ready?" he murmured to Stephanie.

She nodded, her face bleached of color.

"You're doing great." Cole draped his jacket over her thin shoulders.

The tremulous smile that broke through Stephanie's panic brought tears to Grace's eyes.

The girl had been wrapped so tightly in her cocoon of fear and pain that she'd been almost incoherent. But somehow, Cole had accomplished in five minutes what Grace had been trying to do since she'd found Stephanie in the cabin. He'd gotten her to smile.

"Have you ever…delivered a baby?" Stephanie asked they took another shuffling step forward.

"Yup."

She stared at Cole, her pain momentarily forgotten.

"Seriously?"

A smile hooked the corner of his lips. "I wouldn't joke about something like that."

"Let me guess." Grace joined the conversation. "The back of a taxi?"

Cole sent up a silent prayer of thanks that Grace hadn't lost her sense of humor. As Stephanie's labor continued to progress, they were going to have to do everything they could to keep the girl's mind focused on something other than the pain.

"Actually, it was in the parking lot of a McDonald's," he told them.

"I thought that only happened in the…movies," Stephanie said with a rusty chuckle.

"That's what I thought, too." Cole slowed down, matching his stride to Stephanie's as they limped down the path.

"What happened?" Grace positioned herself in front of them, holding up the lantern so they could see where they were going.

"The mom, Vickie, had been feeling tired all day, but didn't know she was in labor because her symptoms didn't sound like the ones she'd read about in her baby book." Cole shook his head.

"By the time she called her husband, her contractions were two minutes apart. He tried to get her to the hospital, but there was an accident during rush hour and the traffic was backed up for two miles. He drove across the median into the parking lot of a McDonald's and called 9-1-1. Guess who got the call? His very first day working as a volunteer for the rescue squad?"

"You," Stephanie guessed.

"That's right. My partner and I were at the gas station a block away when the call came in. Ten minutes later, Vickie gave birth to a healthy baby girl. Eight pounds, six ounces." Cole had been the first person to hold her.

"What did they…name her?"

"Hannah."

"That's pretty." Stephanie's smile faded, and she pressed a hand against her stomach. "Here comes another one."

"Okay." Cole stopped. "Lean on me and breathe. In through your nose, out through your mouth. Like this."

The panic in Stephanie's eyes began to subside as she followed his lead. Cole was never so glad he'd paid attention to those deep-breathing exercises.

"We're almost there." Grace pointed to the cars parked behind the red pine that barricaded the road.

"Do you mind if we take my vehicle?" Cole opened the door of the backseat. "Better gas mileage," he whispered to Stephanie.

He slid a sideways glance at Grace and saw a look of understanding dawn in her eyes. The backseat of his SUV had more room than her pickup. Just in case.

Grace slid behind the wheel and waited for him to get Callie settled.

So far, so good, Lord. Now, how about an ambulance. Or maybe a helicopter.

The trip to the campground seemed to take twice as long. Grace had a viselike grip on the steering wheel as the car bounced down the road.

"Are you sure you don't want to turn around?" Cole called out. "I think you missed a bump back there."

He saw Grace's astonished expression in the rearview mirror and winked at her.

"It's a corduroy road," she said. "The early lumberjacks used to lay down logs so it would be easier to get a team of horses into the woods. If you'd paid attention in history, you would have known that."

"English Lit was my favorite subject," Cole said.

Grace made a sound that could have been a laugh. Or a snort.

"I was always good at math," Stephanie murmured. "I took a few classes at a tech school, and that's when I met Bryce."

The missing boyfriend.

Cole couldn't believe the guy had driven off and left her stranded in a campground. If someone had pulled a stunt like that with Bettina, he'd have more to worry about than a tornado.

"I'm going to see if we have service now and try to call Jake Sutton." Cole fished in his pocket for his cell phone. "He's probably wondering if he should send out a search party to find the search party."

"I think he already did," Grace said.

A squad car, its red-and-blue lights flashing, was coming toward them. The ambulance was right behind it.

Grace pulled over to the side of the road and the squad car stopped a few yards away.

Cole quickly briefed the police chief about the situation. To Sutton's credit, he didn't so much as blink an eye when Cole said they had an eighteen-year-old female in labor.

All he said was, "Of course we do."

The paramedic and EMT from the ambulance were helping Stephanie onto a stretcher when Cole jogged back over to the ambulance.

"They'll take good care of you." He gave her a reassuring smile. "Would you like me to call someone to meet you at the hospital? A friend or family member?"

"No." Pain flashed across Stephanie's face, and Cole had a feeling this one wasn't related to labor.

"Ready?" The ambulance driver poked his head out the window and the paramedic gave him a thumbs-up.

Stephanie grabbed his hand before they could shut the doors. "Thank you, Cole. For everything."

"Take care." He tweaked her nose, a gesture of affection that had always made Bettina smile.

It worked on Stephanie, too.

"Will you tell Grace that I'm glad she was there, too? I don't know what I would have done…without her."

"I'm afraid you're stuck with me a little longer." Grace ducked her head and climbed into the back of the ambulance. "Because I'm coming to the hospital with you."

The smile on Stephanie's face was the last thing Cole saw before the doors closed.

The ambulance pulled away, leaving him standing in the road.

"Grace is pretty amazing."

With a start, Cole realized Jake Sutton was standing beside him.

Grace was more than amazing, Cole thought. She was strong and kind…and he was falling in love with her all over again.

"You look like you could use this."

In the middle of stifling a yawn, Grace could only blink as Kate set a fresh carafe of coffee on the table.

"How is Stephanie doing?" Her friend slid into the chair directly across from her. "Alex and some of the guys stopped in for breakfast about 4:00 a.m. and told me what happened."

Grace didn't have to ask why Kate had been at the café

that early in the morning. She doubted anyone in Mirror Lake had gotten more than a few hours of sleep. Some people in the area had been without electricity for hours as the road crews worked to fix the power lines that had come down. Others chipped in to help neighbors remove trees that had fallen during the storm.

"She had a baby girl less than an hour after she was admitted." Grace smiled. "Stephanie must have miscalculated her due date because the doctor said the baby was full term."

"And you were there for the birth?"

"I couldn't leave her alone," Grace said simply. "We still haven't been able to track down her boyfriend, but Stephanie finally agreed to let me call her parents before I left. Her mom said they were worried sick when Bryce talked Stephanie into going away with him for the weekend. Apparently they'd broken up a few weeks ago and Bryce wanted to convince Stephanie that he'd changed."

Kate topped off their coffee cups. "Cole told Alex he wasn't sure she would make it to the hospital before the baby arrived."

"Neither was I." Grace couldn't prevent a shudder when she remembered how quickly the nurses had moved Stephanie into the delivery room. "But Cole was great. I don't know what we would have done without him."

"That's funny. He said the same thing about you."

"I didn't do anything," Grace protested. "He was the one who kept Stephanie calm."

He'd kept *her* calm, too.

"According to Alex, Cole stayed up all night and pitched in to help. The volunteer rescue squad was maxed out with calls." Kate tipped her head. "Mirror Lake could definitely use a guy with his training."

Grace could see where this was going.

"Cole is probably already on his way back to Madison. His business is there."

Kate was silent for a moment. "I hate to state the obvious, but Alex successfully divides his time between Chicago and Mirror Lake. He still manages Porter Lakeside and drives Abby crazy at the inn."

"That's different. Alex *wants* to be here."

"Maybe Cole does, too."

I want to see you again.

Grace might have believed it if she hadn't overheard that telephone conversation.

"Trust me, Kate. It won't work."

Kate planted her elbows on the table, chin propped in the cradle of her hands. "You and Cole knew each other the summer he lived in Mirror Lake, didn't you?"

Grace couldn't prevent the blush that bloomed in her cheeks.

"I don't know why I didn't see it right away." Kate shook her head. "You two were in love, weren't you?"

Grace couldn't deny that, either.

"Things have changed," she said slowly. "Cole and I are in a different place than we were twelve years ago."

"Maybe it's a *better* place," Kate pointed out. "Both of you are older and wiser. You know what you want now."

Kate might view that as the bridge that would bring her and Cole together, but Grace knew it was the obstacle that would ultimately keep them apart.

Because they wanted different things.

Chapter Nineteen

Grace picked up the stuffed bear that had been occupying the passenger seat of her truck on the drive to the hospital and straightened its plaid bow.

"Don't worry. You're going to like your new home," she murmured.

And the fact that she was talking to a toy proved she could use twelve hours of uninterrupted sleep.

Grace had stumbled into the house after work, changed clothes and got back into the car, anxious to see Stephanie and the baby again. The nurse Grace had talked to during her lunch break had said that both mother and baby were doing fine, but Grace needed to see that for herself.

Stephanie had broken down when her boyfriend hadn't responded to the voice mail she'd left on his phone, letting him know they had a daughter.

It had taken all of Grace's self-control not to leave Bryce a message of her own. Some men seemed to have a problem with responsibility.

An image of Cole teaching Stephanie how to breathe through a contraction flashed through her mind.

She shouldn't have been surprised to discover he'd become a volunteer EMT. He was patient. Caring. The kind of man who would want to give back to the community to honor his father's memory.

Grace blinked back the tears that stung her eyes. Another side effect of sleep deprivation.

The automatic doors swished open as she walked into the spacious front lobby of the hospital.

"Aren't you forgetting something?"

A familiar figure blocked her path and Grace instinctively shifted the bear in her arms, holding it in front of her heart. A flimsy shield against Cole's smile.

"What?" she blurted.

One dark eyebrow lifted. "Me?"

If only that were possible, Grace thought.

"I didn't see your car in the parking lot," she stammered.

Not that she'd looked. Grace had thought for sure Cole had left town after the meetings he'd scheduled with Sloan's attorney and the Realtor.

His gaze dropped to the teddy bear cradled in her arms. "I wanted to buy something for Stephanie and the baby, too, but decided to wait and get your expert opinion."

Grace balked when Cole tried to steer her toward the gift shop. "How did you know I'd be here?"

"Where else would you be?"

Grace wasn't sure how to respond to that. It was a little disturbing that he knew her so well.

"Have you seen Stephanie yet?"

"I just got here a few minutes ago. Sissy had to reschedule our meeting for this afternoon because she wanted to see if the storm had damaged any of her properties."

"Can I help you find something?" A woman wearing a bright pink apron stepped out from behind the counter.

Grace wanted to hug her. Call it denial, but she wasn't ready to hear how Cole's meeting with the Realtor had gone.

"We'll need a dozen roses. Pink." Cole stopped to examine the baby blankets stacked on a shelf. "And two or three of these. And that polka-dot anteater."

"It's an elephant," the clerk said.

"Even better. We'll take it."

"Cole!"

"Every child needs a polka-dot elephant with a yellow bowtie, Grace."

By the time they made their way to the elevator a few minutes later, weighed down with gifts, the clerk was frazzled but beaming.

A young woman wearing Winnie the Pooh scrubs looked up from her computer when they stopped to check in at the nurse's station on the third-floor maternity wing.

"Can I help you?"

"We're here to see Stephanie Swanson," Grace said. "Room 314."

"Just a moment, please." The nurse ducked behind a Plexiglas divider and Grace could see her talking to a gray-haired doctor with a stethoscope looped around his neck.

"What's going on?" Cole murmured.

"I'm not sure."

The nurse returned a few seconds later. "I'm sorry, but Miss Swanson is no longer a patient here."

"What do you mean?" Cole rocked forward and gripped the edge of the counter. "Was she transferred to another hospital?"

"I'm sorry, sir. I'm afraid I'm not at liberty to give out that information."

"I was in the delivery room with Stephanie last night," Grace said. "My name is Grace Eversea."

"Are you a relative?"

"A...friend."

"I'm sorry." A polite smile. "If you'd like to see the baby, she's in the nursery at the end of the hall." The phone on the desk began to ring, and the nurse looked almost relieved by the interruption. "If you'll excuse me…"

"I don't understand." Cole stepped away from the desk and raked a hand through his hair. "If Stephanie is gone, why is the baby still here?"

"Because she decided to put her up for adoption," Grace whispered.

Cole turned to stare at her. "Did Stephanie tell you that?"

Grace's throat closed as pieces of the last conversation she'd had with the teenager began to fall into place.

She's so tiny, Grace.

She's perfect. Grace had cuddled the baby close to her heart, in awe of the tiny fingers and toes. *Do you want to hold her?*

Stephanie had nodded. One more time.

Grace had assumed Stephanie had meant she would hold her daughter one more time before she fell asleep.

"Let's find the nursery." Cole dumped their purchases on the counter and reached for her hand. The warmth of his skin momentarily chased the chill away and Grace was tempted to lean into him. Rest her head against his broad chest and absorb some of his strength.

A girl Stephanie's age shouldn't have to make those kinds of decisions. She should be trying to figure out what college to attend. What to wear for a night out with friends.

The redheaded nurse behind the glass partition was leaning over a bassinet and Grace could see her lips moving as she talked to one of the babies.

"Which one?" Cole asked in a low voice.

The line of bassinet each held a tiny infant, some in pink knit caps, some in blue.

Grace stepped closer to the window and peered through the glass.

To her surprise, the nurse stepped out of the nursery and walked toward them, a baby cradled in her arms.

"I had a feeling you'd be back. I'm Kimberly." The nurse smiled. "We met last night in the delivery room."

"I remember." Grace recognized the woman who'd stayed by Stephanie's side through the entire birth.

"This a good time for a visit. She just woke up."

The baby peered up at her, wide midnight-blue eyes more alert than Grace would have imagined given the fact she'd entered the world only a few hours ago.

"You must be Cole."

"That's right." He looked confused that the nurse knew his name.

"Would you like to hold her?"

"Me?"

The word came out a little louder—okay, maybe a lot louder—than Cole had intended, but the nurse smiled.

"I understand you haven't been formally introduced yet."

Before he could say a word, the baby, as warm as a biscuit straight from the oven and dusted with powder, was deposited in the crook of his arm. He couldn't believe anything could be so...small.

"Hey, munchkin," he murmured.

"Stephanie named her Hannah Grace," Kimberly said softly. "She said you would know why."

Cole knew if he looked at Grace, the tight grip he had on his emotions would begin to unravel. He pressed a kiss against Hannah's petal-soft cheek. "Your turn."

Grace scooped Hannah from his arms with the ease of someone who'd done this before and laughed when the baby's rosebud lips pursed in a frown. "I think she was happy right where she was."

She put her face close to Hannah's, eyes closed, swaying

to a melody no one else could hear. Finally, reluctantly, she gave her back to Kimberly.

"Thank you."

"Thank *you*." The nurse traced the curve of Hannah's cheek. "Stephanie said she didn't know what she would have done if you two hadn't shown up when you did. She's a very special young woman."

All Cole could manage was a quick nod.

Kimberly returned to the nursery and tucked Hannah into the bassinet. Cole dared a look at the woman standing next to him and the tears in her eyes proved to be his undoing. In the middle of the corridor, he folded Grace against his chest and absorbed the tremor that ran through her.

"Sorry." She eased out of his arms and worked up a watery smile. "My coworkers have been telling me for years that eventually I'll develop a tough skin, but I'm still waiting for it to happen."

"I hope you have to wait a long time." Cole hooked a loose strand of silky hair behind her ear. "You *care*, Grace. I would never want you to lose that part of yourself."

"It must have been so difficult for Stephanie to go home without Hannah."

Cole guessed it was going to be difficult for Grace, too.

"Have dinner with me tonight," he said. "I'm not leaving until tomorrow morning."

"I can't. The mayor organized a meeting for the planning committee. He wants to evaluate the celebration."

"One hundred and twenty-five years from now, I vote you leave out the tornado. And the chickens."

"I'll be sure to mention that." Grace smiled but it didn't quite reach her eyes.

"Will you call me when you get home?"

"If it's not too late."

Why did Cole get the feeling it was going to be too late no matter what time the meeting ended?

The elevator door slid open and a silver-haired woman wearing a business suit exited. Her eyes lit up when she spotted Grace.

"I was hoping I hadn't missed you!"

"Cole, this is Doreen Schultz, the hospital social worker," Grace said. "Doreen, Cole Merrick. He's the EMT who helped Stephanie last night."

"The one who almost delivered her baby, if the rumors are correct." Doreen smiled as she shook his hand and then turned back to Grace. "I have to talk to the head nurse, but can you come down to my office in five minutes?"

"Of course."

"It was nice to meet you, Cole." The social worker disappeared into the nursery.

"You don't have to wait for me," Grace said. "The meeting with Doreen could take a while."

Cole knew it wasn't any of his business, but his curiosity got the better of him.

"What does she want you to do?"

Grace's gaze shifted to the window of the nursery and settled on Hannah, already asleep in the bassinet.

"My job."

"Aren't you going to answer that?"

"Not right now." Grace slipped her cell phone back into her purse and hoped Jenna didn't notice that her hand was trembling. "The meeting is about to start."

"In forty-five minutes," Jenna pointed out. "You were here early."

Grace should have known it would raise suspicions. Usually people came up with creative excuses so they could be late for the mayor's "evaluation" meetings. Jenna had spotted Grace hiding—*sitting*—in her truck and pulled into the parking lot to investigate.

It was one of those times when Grace wished her friend wasn't a journalist.

"It was Cole, wasn't it?" Jenna guessed.

"He wants me to stop over at his place after the meeting." The words unfurled with a sigh. "To talk."

"And you're afraid of what he's going to say."

This time Jenna had it wrong. Grace was afraid of what he *was* going to say.

She could no longer deny the attraction between them was mutual. She'd seen it in Cole's eyes. Felt it in his kiss.

I want to see you again.

But he wanted to see Grace, a single professional who would be free to spend time with him when their schedules allowed.

"What's going on?" Jenna prompted. "Everyone could see the sparks flying between you and Cole. To tell you the truth, watching you was more entertaining than the fireworks on Saturday night."

Grace let out a groan. "Don't say that."

"Seriously, is there something you need to talk about?" Jenna flashed a grin. "Off the record, of course."

Grace opened her mouth to tell her that no, everything was fine, and ended up telling her…everything.

How she and Cole had met and fallen in love that summer. How he'd left without a word. Her desire to adopt. Meredith's phone call.

Midway through the storm, Jenna pulled a tissue from her purse.

"I'm okay."

"It's for me." Jenna blew her nose. "I can't believe you didn't tell any of us what you were planning."

"The director at the agency said it could take months for

the adoption to go through. If I'd said anything, Kate and Abby would have been planning a baby shower the next day."

"You're right about that." Jenna chuckled and then her expression turned serious. "But you know we'll be there for you, Grace. The same way all of you were there for me."

No one knew better than Grace, Logan and Tori's social worker, how difficult it had been for Jenna during those first weeks after she'd arrived in Mirror Lake. The children's mother had checked into a drug rehabilitation center after she'd started a fire that damaged the cabin they'd been living in.

Grace had contacted Jenna, who'd agreed to act as temporary guardian to her niece and nephew even though she hadn't seen them for seven years. Jenna, a self-described city girl, had eventually made Mirror Lake her permanent home.

"It could work, you know," Jenna said softly. "A year ago, I thought I had everything I wanted. Now I can't imagine life without Logan and Tori…and Dev. You know he loves those kids like they were his own."

Grace couldn't deny it. The reclusive wildlife photographer, who'd always maintained a careful distance from the rest of the community, was totally committed to his new family.

"It's different."

"How?"

"Cole is focused on his business right now. He lives four hours away from Mirror Lake."

"And he owns a plane," Jenna pointed out with a smile. "I'm not sure I see the problem."

Grace did, but she couldn't break a confidence and tell her friend that Cole had practically raised his siblings during the years their mother had battled depression. Selling his grandfather's property was the only way he could get the funds he needed to expand Painted Skies.

"It will be easier if we don't see each other again."

"Easier on whom? You? Or Cole?"

Jenna did have a way of cutting to the heart of the matter.

"Children aren't part of his plan."

It had taken years for her heart to heal the last time Cole had walked out of her life.

She couldn't go through that again.

Chapter Twenty

"**I**'m sorry you had to cut your visit short, Cole, but Mr. Matheson was quite clear that he wanted *you* to fly him to Saint Louis in the morning. I got the impression he would have taken his business elsewhere if I'd tried to reschedule."

Iola's instincts were probably right, Cole thought grimly. Matheson was the CEO of a software company who expected everything to go a certain way. *His* way.

"You did the right thing." Cole glanced in the rearview mirror and saw a flash of sapphire-blue water, trimmed in gold from the setting sun, before he turned onto the highway.

He'd hoped that he and Grace would have an opportunity to talk, but the mayor's meeting must have gone on longer than she'd expected.

Or she's avoiding you.

Even as Cole shoved that unwelcome thought aside, he couldn't shake the feeling that something was wrong. Even before the storm had hit, he'd felt a chasm opening up between them.

"Hello? Is anyone out there?" Iola's teasing voice intruded on his thoughts.

"Sorry."

"Uh-huh." Iola sounded skeptical. "What happened this

weekend? Usually you're calling me every fifteen minutes, asking for an update. I haven't heard from you all weekend."

"I don't call you every fifteen minutes." It was more like every half hour. "And you wouldn't believe me if I told you."

"The only thing I *wouldn't* believe is that you met someone, fell in love and now Virgil and I will have a new place to go on vacation."

"I'll see you in the morning." Cole was glad Iola couldn't see his expression.

He ended the call and glanced at the digital clock glowing on the dash. It was almost nine, but he decided to leave Grace a brief message, letting her know he was on his way back to Madison.

"Hello?"

"I thought I'd get your voice mail." Just the sound of Grace's voice lifted his spirits. "Is the meeting over?"

"Five minutes ago. I'm walking to the parking lot now."

Cole heard the sound of laughter in the background and found himself wishing he was there. He'd gotten to know her friends over the weekend and it had felt good to laugh with them during the competition. Work beside them in the aftermath of the storm.

Other than his family, Cole had never felt that connected to a group of people. If Grace felt the same way, it was no wonder she'd decided to move back to Mirror Lake after she'd earned her degree.

"Are you on your way home?" he asked.

"I'll be there in about five minutes. You can stop over for a while."

An hour ago, those were the words Cole had been hoping to hear.

"I'd love to…but I'm on my way back to Madison."

"Is everything all right?"

"Something came up at work that I have to deal with. One

of my clients decided to go to Saint Louis at seven o'clock tomorrow morning and I'm the only one who can get him there."

"I didn't realize you were the only one who flew the planes."

Plane, he silently corrected. "Virgil, Iola's husband, helps with the flight school, but he isn't comfortable making long-distance trips anymore. I don't mind because that's my favorite part of the job."

"I see."

It was strange, Cole thought, how two simple words could weigh down a conversation.

"I was thinking I might fly the Cessna to Mirror Lake Saturday when I come up for our dinner date. We could go for a ride after church Sunday."

"About Saturday…I'm afraid something's come up. I'm going to be busy."

"Busy," Cole repeated.

Grace hadn't planned to have this conversation now, but maybe it was better to get it over with. Even though her heart felt like it was going through a shredder.

"What about the following Saturday? Will something come up again?" he added quietly.

"Yes."

The silence that stretched between them made it difficult to breathe.

"What happened, Grace? Are you still holding what I did in the past against me? I'm sorry I wasn't honest with you at the time, but I did what I thought was best."

"This has nothing to do with the past." It was about the future.

"I'm willing to do what it takes to make this work, Grace."

"I'm not." Her throat began to swell shut. "I don't want a long-distance relationship, Cole."

"Alex Porter still works in Chicago."

"But he lives in Mirror Lake."

She heard Cole sigh. "Grace…let's talk about this Saturday. Over dinner."

The husky plea cut through her defenses. Grace was tempted to give in and say yes, but the headlights illuminated something at the end of Sloan's driveway that hadn't been there the last time she'd driven past it.

A "For Sale" sign.

"I don't think that's a good idea. I'm sorry."

"So am I," Cole said tightly. "I'm sorry you're giving up before we have a chance to see where this will lead."

Grace hoped she knew exactly where it would lead.

To the fulfillment of his dream.

"There's someone waiting to see you."

Iola nodded at the door that separated the waiting area from the oversize storage area that housed a rickety desk and a metal filing cabinet.

"In my office?" Cole's eyes narrowed.

No one but family ever sweet-talked their way past his receptionist. Iola considered herself a good judge of character and her opinion was generally based on a potential client's reaction to the vinyl chairs lined up under the window across from her desk. The ones Cole had rescued from the curb one afternoon and bandaged with strips of duct tape.

Cole was downright curious now.

He pushed open the door and his gaze landed on the guy sitting behind the desk. In *his* chair.

"Porter?" A list of possible reasons for Alex's unexpected appearance streaked through Cole's mind and none of them calmed the sudden, erratic beat of his heart. "What are you doing here?"

Alex reached out and idly toyed with the bouquet of Bic

pens that sprouted from a canning jar next to the computer. "I've been in the area on business for a few days, and Thor decided to be difficult. He threw a tantrum on the beltline and left me stranded, so I took a taxi here."

Cole had to ask. "Thor?"

"Kate's Thunderbird." Alex rolled his eyes. "She thought a road trip would be good for the car and me. Bonding time and all that."

Cole tried to picture what that would look like. Alex singing along with the radio? Patting the car's bumper?

"Don't say it," Alex warned.

"Say what?"

"Whatever you were just thinking." Porter rose to his feet and lifted a ceramic mug. The one Bettina had made in her high school ceramics class. The one that said Cole's Cup in bright green letters. "Coffee? Iola made a fresh pot."

Iola didn't make a fresh pot of coffee for him after eight o'clock in the morning, and it was going on two.

"No, thanks." Cole cleared his throat. "I've got a few things to do—"

"Really? Because Iola said you were free the rest of the weekend and I need a ride back to Mirror Lake. Kate is making dinner tonight, and I promised I wouldn't be late."

Cole's mouth dropped open. "You want *me* to take you there? In my plane?"

"Whenever you're ready." Alex tossed back the last sip of coffee and set down the cup.

"From the amount of time you've been waiting, you could have rented a car and been halfway back to there by now," Cole pointed out.

Alex's lips curled up at the corners. If Cole didn't know better, he might—just might—have described it as a smile.

"I didn't think of that."

Cole didn't believe him for an instant. Porter was the

kind of guy who thought about everything. Inside, outside and upside down.

"Sorry, I can't do it."

"Is it because I didn't say the magic word?" Alex shook his head. "I always seem to forget that part."

"Mr. Porter?" Virgil poked his head in the doorway. "I'm all set for your tour."

Cole had no idea they'd started giving tours.

"I'll tag along." He couldn't prevent the sarcasm from leaching into his voice. "If you don't mind."

Alex cuffed Cole on the shoulder as he stalked past. "Not at all."

They followed Virgil into the hangar and Cole tried to stay calm while Alex examined everything from the number of outlets in the wall to the framed newspaper photo of Cole's dad when he'd received an award for heroism after rescuing a woman from a burning building.

And the tour still lasted less than ten minutes.

Alex, however, didn't seem in any hurry to leave. He took a slow lap around the Cessna, leaving Cole with two options. Leave him alone or follow.

Something told him it wasn't a good idea to leave Alex Porter alone.

"How is—" *Grace?* "—everything in town?"

"Almost back to normal."

"And...Kate?"

"I would say she's normal, too, but we both know I'd be exaggerating." There was no hint of criticism embedded in the words, only a deep love for the woman Alex intended to marry.

Cole wrestled down a surge of envy as he ducked under the wing of the plane and checked something he'd already checked twice since his last flight.

"Grace is fine, too," Alex drawled, answering the question Cole hadn't scraped up the courage to ask. "Tired, but I guess that comes with the territory. Kate and Abby have been organizing meals—"

Cole's head jerked up and almost connected with the underside of the wing. "Grace is sick?"

Alex stared at him for a moment. "Kate was right. Again. I'm never going to hear the end of it," he muttered. "Grace didn't tell you."

"Tell me what? I haven't talked to her since—" *she broke our date and told me she didn't want to see me again* "—I left town two weeks ago."

Porter hesitated, which only increased the fear swirling in Cole's gut. Alex wasn't the type of guy who struggled to find the right words.

"She's been busy," he finally said. "With the baby."

Cole couldn't have heard him right. "Grace doesn't have a baby."

"She does now. You know Stephanie chose adoption?"

Cole nodded. "I found out when we went to visit her the next day."

"Grace took Hannah home from the hospital until she's placed in a permanent home."

Cole remembered the hospital social worker who'd asked Grace to meet with her.

Something came up, she'd said on the phone the last time they'd spoken.

Grace must have known that Hannah would be with her. So why hadn't she simply explained the situation?

Cole grabbed his clipboard with the preflight checklist. "I'll have the plane ready in an hour."

Chapter Twenty-One

Grace had been on autopilot for the last half hour, walking the floors and counting the animals in the ark on the wallpaper border until green giraffes and blue kangaroos danced in her head.

She heard a soft rap on the front door and started down the stairs.

"One of your admirers is here, sweetie." Grace dropped a kiss on the tiny face peeking out from the petals of the pink blanket.

Jenna had mentioned she was going to stop over for a few minutes to drop off a "little something." All of Grace's friends had been in and out the past few days, bringing meals and gifts. Arguing over who got to hold Hannah. Right now, they were the only people allowed to see her like this. Sleep-deprived. Wearing sweatpants and a T-shirt that smelled like baby powder.

She winced when she saw the pile of freshly laundered towels on the sofa that needed to be folded.

"Come in." Grace raised her voice a notch above the lullaby drifting from the miniature speakers set up on the coffee table, a present from Zoey and Matt.

The front door opened and closed with a soft click.

"Things are a little chaotic at the mo—" Grace's heart buckled when Cole sauntered into the living room.

He looked…amazing. A heather-gray shirt that set off his eyes. Faded jeans and a lightweight jacket embroidered with the Painted Skies logo.

It wasn't fair that he smelled good, too.

While she stared at him, speechless, he padded toward her, his eyes focused on the baby in her arms. A split second later, her arms were empty and Cole was cradling Hannah against the strong plane of his chest.

It didn't cross Grace's mind to protest.

"Hey, there, peanut." His voice rumbled out, as soft and soothing as the chenille blanket she'd wrapped around Hannah after her bath.

"What are you doing here?" Grace blurted.

"We have a dinner date, remember?"

A dinner date two weeks ago. And one she distinctly remembered *canceling*.

"I can't go anywhere." Grace clutched a pillow against her stomach to hide a stain on the front of her shirt.

Cole tossed a smile her way. "I stopped on the way here and ordered a pizza. Deluxe, extra cheese, no mushrooms."

Grace's stomach rumbled. "Is it hot?"

"Guaranteed or your money back." Cole grinned and she closed her eyes. A poor defense against his irresistible charm, but she was tired.

And way too happy to see him.

Grace's gaze narrowed on the brightly colored package in his hand.

"Who told you?"

Cole didn't have to ask what she meant. "Porter paid me a visit earlier this afternoon."

"*Alex?*" Grace choked out. She'd made her friends promise that no one would interfere with her decision, but it hadn't crossed her mind to extract one from their significant others.

"He got stranded in Madison and asked me to fly him back for the dinner. He said you've been busy with the baby. But that leads to another question. Why didn't *you* tell me?"

Guilt pinched her conscience. "Everything happened so fast."

It was a lame excuse and she could tell she hadn't fooled Cole. His next question confirmed it.

"You offered to take Hannah the day you met with the social worker, didn't you?"

"Hannah was being released from the hospital and needed a place to go." Grace sat down on the sofa and tucked her bare feet beneath her. "I was the logical choice. Stephanie is going through a private adoption agency and it's important to her that she meet the couple who wants to adopt Hannah. That's why the process is taking a little longer than usual."

Cole looked down at Hannah with a tenderness that made Grace's heart ache. "She's bigger."

"She's a sweetie. She eats well and gets up only a few times a night."

"Who watches her during the day?"

"I took a leave of absence from work."

She saw the flicker of surprise in Cole's eyes before he could hide it. "How long do you think she'll be with you?"

Not long enough. "I'm not sure."

"Is Hannah the reason you canceled our dinner date?"

Grace knotted her hands together in her lap. "I'm not interested in a long-distance relationship, remember?"

Cole regarded her steadily. "That's what you told me."

But he didn't believe her.

"It won't...work."

"Why not? We can still see each other on the weekends. I'll help with Hannah while she's here."

She knew he would help. That was the problem. But Cole thought the situation was temporary. It was one thing to devote a few hours to caring for a child…another to make a child part of your life.

"I think I heard Jenna's car." Grace vaulted to her feet and practically sprinted to the front door. "I'll be right back."

It snapped shut behind her.

"That went well." Cole looked down at Hannah. "I think she's coming around. But feel free to put a good word in for me, okay?"

"'Kay."

Cole slowly lifted his head. A little boy with tousled blond hair and enormous cinnamon brown eyes stood a few feet away, clutching the polka-dot elephant he had bought for Hannah in the hospital gift shop.

"Hi," Cole said cautiously.

The boy scrambled onto the sofa and stared at him. "Who're you?"

"I'm Cole."

"I'm this many." The boy carefully pressed down his thumb and pinkie and held up three fingers.

"Three," Cole repeated solemnly. "You're a big boy."

He was rewarded with a bright smile. "Hannah sleeping."

Cole glanced down at the baby nestled in the crook of his arm and then at the boy clad in race car pajamas. "It must be past her bedtime. Are *you* supposed to be sleeping?"

"Nope."

"Sorry it took so long. The pizza delivery guy pulled in right behind Jenna…" Grace braked in the middle of the room when she spotted them.

"No problem," Cole said easily. "We were just getting acquainted, weren't we?"

"I'm hungry." The boy slid off the sofa and padded toward

her, his straight little nose twitching as the aroma of melted cheese permeated the air.

"You're always hungry." Grace tickled his belly and he giggled. "Why don't you build a tower for me while I set the table, sweetie?"

"Okay." He upended a basket of wooden blocks and plunked down in the middle of them.

Cole remembered his brothers doing the same thing and smiled. He looked at Grace. "So, who's your friend?"

She hesitated for a fleeting moment and then smiled back. "His name is Michael."

"You're still here."

Grace paused on the bottom step as Cole finished folding the last of the towels.

"Where did you think I'd go?"

Her gaze shifted to the door and the small but telling gesture landed like a kick to his solar plexus.

Right. He supposed some guys would have taken off the minute her back was turned, but Cole needed some answers. They hadn't had an opportunity to talk after she'd dropped that bombshell on him. The phone had started to ring, Michael's block tower had fallen over and Hannah decided it was time for her bottle. All within the space of sixty seconds.

Cole helped Michael rebuild the tower while Grace fed Hannah. They'd munched on cold pizza and when she'd put the kids to bed, he'd picked up the toys scattered around the living room.

"You probably have things to do." She lingered at the bottom of the staircase. "I shouldn't keep you."

"Not really." *And yes, you should.*

Grace finally ventured into the living room, pausing to fluff a pillow that didn't need to be fluffed. Brushing an invisible piece of lint from a cushion.

Cole couldn't stand to see her so uncertain. A week ago, she'd been at his side, in his arms, and he had no idea what to do or say to cross the distance between them.

"So…Hannah and Michael are both waiting to be adopted?" he ventured.

"Michael's adoption was finalized two days ago," Grace said softly.

"Then why is he with you?"

"Because I'm the one who adopted him."

Cole didn't think it was possible, but she'd shocked him all over again.

Grace sank into the closest chair and turned to face him. "Under the Safe Haven law, babies can be left at a hospital or police or fire station up to seventy-two hours after they're born and the parents won't face prosecution for abandonment."

Cole's stomach twisted as the words sank in. "Michael?"

"He was several weeks premature, so he spent a month in the NICU until his lungs were fully developed. After that, he was placed in temporary foster care that turned out to not be so temporary because he had some minor health issues.

"The couple whom Michael lived with considered adopting him, but changed their minds when they found out recently they were going to have twins." Grace reached between the sofa cushions and smiled as she pulled out a plastic truck. "That's when Meredith, the director of a private adoption agency, called me."

"Hasn't it been difficult for Michael to adjust to a new home? To you?"

"Meredith brought him over for a few hours every day this week so we could get to know each other. He moved in Thursday and so far, he's been doing remarkably well. They both are."

"How did this happen so fast?" Cole frowned. "I thought the adoption process could take a while."

"It wasn't fast." Grace's lips tipped in a rueful smile. "I've been on the waiting list for months."

She'd been *planning* to adopt.

Cole tried to wrap his mind around the news.

"I know what you're thinking." Grace sighed. "My parents and my older sister said the same thing. I'm going to have a hard time letting Hannah go when the time comes."

"You will," Cole agreed, "but that's not what I was thinking. I was thinking that one of the things I love about you is that you're one of those people who has the courage to say yes."

Grace stared at him—and promptly burst into tears.

It wasn't quite the response Cole expected.

He followed his instincts and pulled her into his arms. Smiled when he caught a whiff of baby powder mingling with the familiar scent of lilacs.

When the storm began to subside, with it came the knowledge that he didn't want to let her go.

"I'm sorry," Grace told his shirt pocket.

"Don't apologize. Sleep deprivation isn't easy on anyone and you're adjusting to a lot of changes, like any new mom. Things will get easier."

She blinked up at him. "When?"

Cole thought about Bettina and the twins. "In about fifteen years."

A smile shimmered in Grace's eyes. She drew back a few inches, putting some distance between them.

"I better go to bed or Hannah will wake up right when I'm about to fall asleep."

The enormity of what she'd taken on—alone—suddenly hit him.

A newborn baby and an active toddler.

Cole remembered the times he'd been overwhelmed taking care of his siblings. The nights he'd fallen asleep on top of the blankets because he'd been too tired to crawl between them. The nights he'd played flashlight tag with his brothers and read Bettina's favorite fairy tale over and over, wearing the paper crown she'd made him.

He missed it.

The house was clean. He had the evenings to himself. And all he'd felt over the past two weeks was a yawning emptiness. He'd found himself missing Grace more than he'd thought was possible. And he missed his family.

"What time is the service tomorrow morning?"

Grace's forehead puckered. "Nine, but—"

"I'll be here at eight-thirty."

He showed up at eight. With warm cinnamon rolls from the café and a cup of black coffee that cleared the cobwebs from Grace's brain before she even took a sip.

Grace tried to avoid the knowing looks on her friends' faces when she and Cole walked into church with the children, but knew it was only a matter of time before one—or six—of them came over to say hello. It didn't help that Hannah and Michael drew a crowd wherever they went.

Zoey had managed to coax Michael to come with her to the nursery by mentioning the new slide, so Grace had placed him in her friend's capable hands.

"Hey, cutie." Abby neatly removed the baby from her arms as the opening prelude started. "And Grace. And Cole."

"We're having a potluck after church today." Kate eased in next to Abby. "You're staying, right?"

"I didn't bring anything to contribute, and Hannah and Michael take a nap right after lunch."

"That's the beauty of a potluck." Emma had joined the

ranks, the three of them forming a formidable wall of women who weren't going to take no for an answer. "There's plenty of food and you can leave right afterward. No cleanup."

Grace was relieved when the prelude ended, a cue for Matt to greet the congregation. Abby reluctantly returned Hannah and Kate's parting smile promised the conversation wasn't over.

"You know we won't be able to leave the parking lot until we've eaten our weight in pasta salad, right?" Cole murmured.

Grace tried to ignore the flutter the word *we* stirred inside her chest.

"You can stay," she told him. "I'm sure there are people you'd like to talk to."

Like Sissy Perkins. And Marty Sullivan.

Cole gave her the look she was beginning to recognize. "We rode in the same car. You're stuck with me."

"Faye McAllister was right," Grace whispered. "You do have a stubborn chin."

He winked at her, as if she'd just paid him a compliment.

It was the first time in years that Grace hadn't been able to concentrate on one of Matt's sermons. Cole was so close that every time she took a breath, she inhaled the fresh scent of soap and freshly laundered cotton. Her one hope was that Hannah would raise a ruckus so she would have to take her out of the sanctuary, but the baby refused to cooperate and slept through the majority of the service.

By the time Matt closed in prayer, Grace was ready to bolt. She buckled Hannah into her infant seat and reached for the diaper bag.

Cole had already slung it over his arm. On anyone else, pink and lavender bunnies would have looked comical. On Cole, they only made him look more masculine. And handsome.

And she was in so much trouble....

"Look!" Michael, waving a piece of paper, bypassed her and tumbled into Cole's arms. "I gotta plane."

"Michael picked out that page to color," Zoey murmured. "And I told him that Cole flew planes."

He also saved lives and folded towels and could turn a woman's heart upside down with one smile.

"I would *kill* Alex," she muttered, "if I knew it wouldn't upset Kate."

"Don't blame him. The vote was unanimous." Zoey grinned. "Alex was the only person we figured could get away with it."

The vote?

"I'm moving to New York City. Where no one knows me."

"Not until you have a piece of cake. Which reminds me, I better help Kate and Abby finish setting up." Zoey laughed and scooted away.

Cole didn't talk to Sissy Perkins or Marty Sullivan. He talked to Michael. Rocked Hannah to sleep. Brought Grace a piece of white cake when all the other women around the table were eating chocolate.

People drifted over to say hello while they ate and Grace braced herself for the curious looks. The questions. But no one seemed the least bit surprised that she and Cole were together.

Grace found that a little disturbing.

The fresh air and sunshine worked its magic and Hannah began to fuss a little.

Cole leaned over and his breath whispered against her ear. "Time to go home?"

Grace managed a nod, her only way of communicating because she'd suddenly lost the ability to speak. Again.

Cole wasn't part of her life. He couldn't be.

Every time hope began to stir, Grace extinguished them with the words she'd heard him say.

My days of raising children are over.

And hers were just beginning.

Chapter Twenty-Two

The bells above the door jingled as Cole walked into the Grapevine café Monday morning.

Kate waved to him behind the counter.

"I got your message. You wanted to talk to me?"

"Not me." Kate flashed a wide smile. "Him."

Cole turned around and saw Alex Porter sitting in a corner booth.

"Why do I get the feeling I've been set up?"

"Because you're an intelligent man." Kate handed him a cup of coffee. "Now go."

Cole slid into the vinyl bench opposite Alex.

"You didn't tell me about Michael," he said without preamble.

"I was out of town on business." Porter shrugged. "The last time I talked to Kate, Grace only had one. Does it matter?"

It was a question Cole had asked himself a hundred times since he'd knocked on Grace's door Saturday night. And he kept coming up with the same answer.

"No."

Alex's expression didn't change, but Cole had the impression he'd said the right thing. "Did you know that Kate was

Logan and Tori Gardner's foster mom before Jenna arrived in Mirror Lake?"

"Grace didn't mentioned that."

"It doesn't happen very often, but Kate takes in children in emergency situations. Something I found out when we managed Abby's inn last summer." Alex paused, his faint smile obviously triggered by a memory. "The kids moved in with her while Grace tried to locate Jenna, their only living relative. I knew if they didn't find her, Kate would have moved mountains to make sure Logan and Tori ended up with her permanently."

"Did you have second thoughts about pursuing a relationship with Kate?"

"Not for a minute. By that time, I knew without a doubt that God had brought Kate into my life. And that meant whatever came along with her...a town with fifteen-hundred people...two annoying cats, foster children...I figured those things were part of God's plan for me, too."

Cole felt a new respect for Porter. And suddenly he understood how the guy had managed to win Kate's heart.

"I care about Grace," Cole said. "I want to be part of her life, but I'm not sure she wants me anymore." He hadn't realized how hard it would be to admit.

"Maybe this isn't about what she wants," Alex said. "What does she think *you* want?"

"To expand Painted Skies." Cole didn't hesitate. It was all he'd talked about. The reason he'd wanted to sell a piece of property that had been in his family for over a hundred years.

"And where would a family fit into that plan?" Alex asked. "Because Grace is part of a package deal now."

"I don't think you fit a family into your plan. They become the plan and everything else fits around..."

"Them," Alex finished.

Bits and pieces of the conversation he'd had with Grace at the fireworks began to come back to him.

For the first time I can concentrate on Painted Skies... there were things I couldn't do while I split my time and attention between my family and the business.

"She thinks she and Michael will get in the way of what I want," Cole said.

"Knowing Grace, that would be my guess."

"So how am I supposed to convince Grace that *she's* what I want?"

"I have no idea."

"Now you're telling me you don't have all the answers?" Cole was only half joking.

"Yes, but don't let that get around." Alex didn't crack a smile. "I made some stupid mistakes and almost lost Kate because of them."

"What did you do to win her back?"

"Dived into a nest of hornets, went into anaphylactic shock and ended up in the hospital. Canceled a dinner party behind her back and then showed up at her apartment with an engagement ring. But I wouldn't recommend that route." Alex's lips twisted in a smile. "It's not for amateurs."

Under different circumstances, Cole would have been tempted to smile back.

"I think Grace is afraid I'll change my mind about us and walk away."

"That's it, then."

Cole decided he must have missed something. "What's it?"

"If she's worried you're going to leave...then stay."

The door of the café swung open and a tall, fair-haired man wearing plaid golf pants and a bright yellow polo strode toward them.

"Sorry I'm late."

"You should be," Alex growled. "Cole, this is Jeff Gaines. He owns a resort and condominiums north of town. Most of his guests are businessmen who need a place to unwind for the weekend."

Cole nodded politely, anxious to get back to his conversation with Alex.

"It's nice to finally meet you, Cole." Gaines slid into the booth. "Let's get to it, okay? The senator and I tee off at eleven."

Cole glanced at Alex. "Get down to what?"

Porter smiled.

"Expanding your business."

Grace heard the sound of an engine and when she peeked out the window, she saw Cole on a riding lawn mower, carving a path through the grass near the horse pen.

"What is he doing?" she muttered.

Michael pattered over to the window and pressed his palms against the glass.

"Cole!"

In response to his enthusiastic shout, Hannah kicked her chubby legs and gurgled.

Grace was outnumbered.

It was Wednesday morning and Cole was still in Mirror Lake. On Monday, he'd brought Michael a tricycle and then showed him how to ride it while she'd put the baby down for her nap. On Tuesday, he'd talked her into going on a short walk. To the place they'd met. Grace sat on the hammock-shaped rock with Hannah cradled in her arms and watched Cole and Michael wade up to their ankles, chasing silver minnows through the shallow water.

Every morning, Grace told herself that Cole wouldn't show up at the door. But she hoped he would. Every moment she spent with Cole made her want one more. And another. Until all those moments added up to forever.

"Can I go outside and play now?"

"After your nap, we'll walk down to the barn and give B.C. some apple slices." Grace turned away from the window, glad for the distraction.

"I'm not—" he yawned "—sleepy."

"I'll read you a story after I put Hannah in her crib," Grace said, knowing Michael would be sound asleep by the time she reached the end of the book.

Half an hour later, she backed out of Michael's bedroom and closed the door, then checked on Hannah. Over the past few days, they'd slipped into a routine. Grace worked part-time from home in the evenings, an answer to prayer because she didn't want to leave Michael and Hannah with a sitter during the day.

If only she knew what to do about Cole.

A breeze carried the scent of freshly mowed grass through the open window and Grace realized she hadn't heard the sound of the lawn mower in a while.

She peeked out the window and saw Cole standing by the round pen, having what looked to be a serious conversation with B.C.

The mare butted his arm, a gesture of affection reserved only for close friends and family.

Now, Grace thought wryly, it was three against one. Cole had won everyone over.

His head suddenly swiveled in her direction and Grace didn't have time to duck behind the curtain.

The next thing she knew, he was walking up to the house with that easy, confident stride that made it look as if he belonged in her yard. In her life.

Grace met him on the porch, hands planted on her hips.

"Why are you still here?"

Cole tucked his hands in his front pockets. "You want me to leave?"

"No...*yes*."

Laughter danced in the cedar-green eyes. "I'm glad you cleared that up."

"You're neglecting your business."

"No, I'm not."

"How can you say that?" she snapped. "You're in Mirror Lake. Your business is in Madison."

Cole smiled. "One of them is."

Grace paced the length of the porch. "You shouldn't be here. The house is sold and—"

"Who told you that?" Cole interrupted.

Grace stopped pacing. "The For Sale sign is gone."

"That's because I took it off the market."

Grace's eyes widened in shock and Cole couldn't prevent a smile.

Thank You, Lord.

He'd been praying for an opportunity to talk to her and it looked like this was it.

"Why don't you sit down?" he suggested.

Grace sat.

Cole dropped into the wicker chair opposite hers and pulled in a slow breath, searching for the right words.

"When I told you about my family the night we went to the fireworks, I left something out.

"When my mom shut down, Sean and Travis started acting up at school. Honestly, I thought they were going to get kicked out of first grade." Cole shook his head at the memory. "Bettina cried a lot. I kept telling myself that Mom would feel better in a few days. But then a few days went by...and then a few months."

It was difficult to revisit the past, but Cole pressed on because he knew the future—their future—was at stake.

"On graduation day, I called the florist and ordered a dozen roses. For you, Grace. I was going to drive to Mirror Lake and surprise you. I know it sounds crazy. I hadn't written or called you for months. But my feelings for you hadn't changed…and I was hoping, praying, that yours hadn't, either.

"But then Sean fell off the monkey bars that morning and needed stitches. Because of what happened to Dad, Mom couldn't deal with the emergency room, so I loaded up Bettina and the boys and took them to the hospital. When we got home, Mom was gone. I finally found her, three hours later, sitting on a bench in the park. And I knew my family needed me. I was in this for the long haul and it wouldn't be fair to pull you into it."

"I still think you should have told me," Grace whispered. "You should have given me the opportunity to decide."

Cole released a slow breath and sent up a silent prayer that he was doing the right thing.

"You didn't."

Grace stiffened. "What are you talking about?"

"I'm guessing you decided I should have my freedom after spending the last twelve years taking care of my family. That's why you broke our date and told me that you didn't want to see me anymore. It wasn't because you didn't have feelings for me. You assumed that when I found out you wanted to adopt a baby, I'd walk away."

"No." Grace finally met his gaze. "It was because I was afraid you *wouldn't.* You're a good man, Cole. I knew you'd want to help with Hannah. And I was right. You're here, changing diapers and mowing the lawn and playing with Michael when you should be putting in the hours at Painted Skies. I can't ask you to give up something you've worked so hard for. Something that means so much to you."

"When I found out about Sloan's will, I thought God had opened a door. Blessed the work of my hands. Later, I thought He wanted me to make peace with the past. But now I know He was giving me another chance at a future. With *you*. Because I can't imagine anywhere else I'd rather be."

"But you said your days of raising children were over. I heard you."

The telephone conversation he'd had with Bettina instantly downloaded in his mind, and Cole groaned.

"I was *teasing* her, Grace."

She didn't look convinced.

"I've been talking to Alex the past few days. He and his friend, Jeff Gaines, want me to operate another branch of Painted Skies north of Mirror Lake. Most of Gaines's clients are businessmen who would rather charter a plane than spend six hours in the car to come up here for a weekend of golf or fishing. And Alex claims he can spend more time with Kate if he can make the trip to Chicago and back in a day.

"I already talked to Virgil and Iola. They're willing to run the flight school and they gave me the name of a pilot who might be interested in making the longer trips." Cole was still reeling from the phone call he'd gotten from his former boss the night before. He'd never imagined Cap would find retirement boring, but he was anxious to get back in the cockpit again.

"That's why you stayed in Mirror Lake?" Grace looked stunned. "You were planning all this?"

"Not exactly." He grinned when her eyes darkened with confusion. "I've been pursuing *you*."

"Pursuing me?" she repeated.

"Trying to get you to fall madly in love with me." Cole leaned forward. "The way I love you. Now the only question I have for you is…is it working?"

"No."

Cole's heart dropped to his feet. "No?"

She leaned forward until they were inches apart. Smiled. "You accomplished that twelve years ago."

Epilogue

"I need your opinion." Grace dipped a wooden spoon in the mixing bowl and offered it to Cole.

He ignored it and brushed a kiss against her lips instead. "Perfect."

Grace laughed. "I meant the frosting. Is it sweet enough?"

"Not as sweet as you."

"Don't you have something to do?" she said with mock exasperation.

"I'm watching you. That's something."

"You're *distracting* me."

Cole grinned, not the least bit repentant. "How is the birthday girl?"

"Wonderful." Grace nudged him to the side and spread a layer of frosting on the cake she'd baked that morning. He reached for her again and she went willingly into his arms…until the slam of a car door signaled the arrival of their first guests.

"Kate and Abby," she guessed. Her friends had offered to come to the house a few minutes early to help with last-minute preparations for the party.

Cole swiped the tip of his finger against the side of the bowl before he followed her outside.

"Mama!" Michael raced toward them, their one-year-old chocolate lab at his heels. "Me an' Aunt Bettina taught Pilot a new trick."

Cole's sister followed at a more leisurely pace. "What took you so long, big brother?" she teased. "You said you'd only be gone a minute."

Cole reached out and tugged on the end of his sister's ponytail as if she were still a mischievous six-year-old. "I got a little…distracted."

"Uh-huh." Grace blushed when Bettina gave her a knowing look.

Michael wrapped his arms around Cole's leg. "Do you wanna see, Daddy?"

"Of course I do."

Grace's throat tightened and she blinked away a mist of tears. Michael had become Cole's shadow and she knew he wouldn't have it any other way.

"Hi, Kate! Hi, Abby!" Bettina ambled toward the women. She glanced over her shoulder and flashed a teasing smile at Cole. "Don't get distracted again!"

"Are you sure you want her to stay with us for a few weeks?" he murmured.

"I'm sure. I love your family."

"They love you." He lowered his voice. "And so do I, Mrs. Merrick."

Grace never got tired of hearing the words. They'd exchanged vows near the pond on Cole's property the previous summer and moved into the brick house after a brief honeymoon. Cole had finished the patio and a trio of new handprints were lined up next to his father's in the concrete.

"The decorating committee is here!" Kate pulled a bouquet of colorful balloons from the backseat of her car.

More cars pulled into the driveway and soon the yard was filled with people.

Cole looked around. "Aren't we missing someone?"

"Here is the birthday girl!" Cole's mother, Debra, stepped onto the porch and Grace started laughing.

Hannah, in a pink sundress and a sparkly tiara, scrambled down from her grandmother's arms and toddled over to Cole.

"How about it, princess?" He scooped her up. "Ready to say hello to your guests?"

Hannah bobbed her head. "Dada."

"Mama," he quickly corrected with a sideways glance at Grace.

"Don't bother." Grace chuckled. "I've heard you coaching her."

The party officially started when Hannah blew out the single birthday candle on her cake. Sean and Travis, Cole's brothers, had set up a volleyball net and the younger adults formed teams while others took a walk down to the lake or sat in the shade and visited.

Grace watched Hannah romping in the grass with Pilot, her tiara already askew. Michael was chasing a ball with one of his friends from Sunday school.

Cole wrapped his arm around her waist and Grace leaned against him.

"Meredith said the paperwork is ready to sign," she murmured. "In a week, Amber Lynn will be moving in with us. Are you sure we can handle one more?"

She saw the answer in Cole's eyes and her heart swelled with love even before he said the word.

"Yes."

* * * * *

Dear Reader,

Thank you for visiting Mirror Lake! I hope you enjoyed connecting with "old" friends and making some new ones.

While writing this book, I thought about all the times I've tried to figure out God's plan. Years ago, when I first started writing, a publisher contacted me about submitting a book of devotions for their consideration. I was sure God was opening a door—until a letter arrived shortly after I submitted my idea. The editor liked it but felt my writing style was more suited to fiction. I was disappointed and confused... but then I realized I had always loved writing fiction. And more specifically, inspirational romance! If not for that letter and the realization that God might be pointing me in a different direction, I might not have written *Tested by Fire*, my debut novel for Love Inspired.

Cole was convinced that God had led him to Mirror Lake to sell the family home, but discovers He had another plan all along. Things didn't look the way Cole had imagined either, but in the end, he realized God's plan is the best. I hope you believe that, too!

Please visit my website at kathrynspringer.com and say hello. I'd love to hear from you!

Keep smiling and seeking Him!

Kathryn Springer

Questions for Discussion

1. What were your dreams and goals when you were in high school? How did they change over the years?

2. What modern convenience would you have a difficult time giving up?

3. Have you ever traced your family history? Who or what was the most fascinating person or fact you discovered?

4. Just for fun, if you could journey back in time, what year would you choose? Why?

5. Cole and Grace were paired together for a fun competition during the town's 125th birthday celebration. Which item would you have chosen if you'd been in their place? What do you think the most challenging part of life would have been for settlers in 1887?

6. Did you agree with Cole's reason for leaving Grace behind? Why or why not?

7. Grace and her friends work together to build a shelter. How is this symbolic? Who has been your "shelter" when you've been in difficult situations?

8. What do you think verse nine in Proverbs 16 means? *"In his heart a man plans his course, but the Lord determines his steps."* Discuss.

9. At the end of the book, Cole's dream to expand his business didn't look the way he thought it would. Has something similar happened to you? Describe the situation.

10. What was your favorite scene?

11. Grace and Cole discovered that some of the decisions they'd made for their future were the result of the influence they'd had on each other in the past. Has someone in your past had a strong impact on your life? In what way?

12. What happened in Grace and Cole's life in the twelve years they were apart that prepared them for a future together?

13. What qualities did you see in Cole that made him a good match for Grace?

14. Cole's grandfather left him a house and property as an inheritance, but Matt Wilde encourages him to leave a legacy. What is the difference? What kind of legacy do you want to leave your family?

15. What have you had the courage to say "yes" to over the years?

REQUEST YOUR FREE BOOKS!

2 FREE INSPIRATIONAL NOVELS
PLUS 2
FREE
MYSTERY GIFTS

Love Inspired

YES! Please send me 2 FREE Love Inspired® novels and my 2 FREE mystery gifts (gifts are worth about $10). After receiving them, if I don't wish to receive any more books, I can return the shipping statement marked "cancel." If I don't cancel, I will receive 6 brand-new novels every month and be billed just $4.49 per book in the U.S. or $4.99 per book in Canada. That's a saving of at least 22% off the cover price. It's quite a bargain! Shipping and handling is just 50¢ per book in the U.S. and 75¢ per book in Canada.* I understand that accepting the 2 free books and gifts places me under no obligation to buy anything. I can always return a shipment and cancel at any time. Even if I never buy another book, the two free books and gifts are mine to keep forever.

105/305 IDN FVV7

Name _____ (PLEASE PRINT)

Address _____ Apt. #

City _____ State/Prov. _____ Zip/Postal Code

Signature (if under 18, a parent or guardian must sign)

Mail to the **Harlequin® Reader Service:**
IN U.S.A.: P.O. Box 1867, Buffalo, NY 14240-1867
IN CANADA: P.O. Box 609, Fort Erie, Ontario L2A 5X3

Are you a subscriber to Love Inspired books and want to receive the larger-print edition?
Call 1-800-873-8635 or visit www.ReaderService.com.

* Terms and prices subject to change without notice. Prices do not include applicable taxes. Sales tax applicable in N.Y. Canadian residents will be charged applicable taxes. Offer not valid in Quebec. This offer is limited to one order per household. Not valid for current subscribers to Love Inspired books. All orders subject to credit approval. Credit or debit balances in a customer's account(s) may be offset by any other outstanding balance owed by or to the customer. Please allow 4 to 6 weeks for delivery. Offer available while quantities last.

Your Privacy—The Harlequin® Reader Service is committed to protecting your privacy. Our Privacy Policy is available online at www.ReaderService.com or upon request from the Harlequin Reader Service.

We make a portion of our mailing list available to reputable third parties that offer products we believe may interest you. If you prefer that we not exchange your name with third parties, or if you wish to clarify or modify your communication preferences, please visit us at www.ReaderService.com/consumerschoice or write to us at Harlequin Reader Service Preference Service, P.O. Box 9062, Buffalo, NY 14269. Include your complete name and address.

LI13

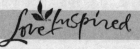
Jolie followed Morgan outside. There was a large gnarled oak tree still bent over as it had been all those years ago. She didn't stop until she reached it, turning his way only after they were beneath the wide expanse of limbs.

Morgan crossed his arms and studied the tree. "I remember having to climb up this tree and talk you down after you scrambled up to the top and froze."

She hadn't expected him to bring up old memories—it caught her a little off guard. "I remember how mad you were at having to rescue the silly little new girl."

A hint of a smile teased his lips, fraying Jolie's nerves at the edges. It had been a long time since she'd seen that smile.

"I got used to it, though," he said, his voice warming.

Electricity hummed between them as they stared at each other. Jolie sucked in a wobbly breath. Then the hardness in Morgan's tone matched the accusation in his eyes.

"What are you doing here, Jolie? Why aren't you taming rapids in some far off place?"

"I...I'm—" She stumbled over her words. "I'm taking a leave from competition for a little while. I had a bad run in Virginia." She couldn't bring herself to say that she'd almost died. "Your dad offered me this teaching opportunity."

"I heard about the accident and I'm real sorry about that, Jolie," Morgan said. "But why come here after all this time?"

"This is my *home*."

Jolie saw anger in Morgan's eyes. Well, he had a right to it, and more than a right to point it straight at her.

But she'd thought she'd prepared for it.

She was wrong.

"Morgan," Jolie said, almost as a whisper. "I'd hoped we could forget the past and move forward."

Heart pounding, she reached across the space between them and placed her hand on his arm. It was just a touch, but the feeling of connecting with Morgan McDermott again after so much time rocked her straight to her core, and suddenly she wasn't so sure coming home had been the right thing to do after all.

Will Morgan ever allow Jolie back into
his life—and his heart?

Pick up HER UNFORGETTABLE COWBOY
available May 2013 from Love Inspired Books.

LIEXP0413

Will You Marry Me?

Bold widow Johanna Yoder stuns Roland Byler when she asks him to be her husband. To Johanna, it seems very sensible that they marry. She has two children, he has a son. Why shouldn't their families become one? But the widower has never forgotten his long-ago love for her; it was his foolish mistake that split them apart. This could be a fresh start for both of them—until she reveals she wants a marriage of convenience only. It's up to Roland to woo the stubborn Johanna and convince her to accept him as her groom in her home and in her heart.

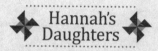

Hannah's
Daughters

Johanna's Bridegroom

by

Emma Miller

Available May 2013

www.LoveInspiredBooks.com

LI8781

Love Inspired HISTORICAL

In the fan-favorite miniseries
Cowboys of Eden Valley

LINDA FORD

presents

The Cowboy's Convenient Proposal

Second Chance Ranch

She is a woman in need of protection. But trust is the one thing feisty Grace "Red" Henderson is sure she'll never give any man again—not even the cowboy who rescued her. Still, Ward Walker longs to protect the wary beauty and her little sister—in all the ways he couldn't safeguard his own family.

Red desperately wants to put her tarnished past behind her. Little by little, Ward is persuading her to take a chance on Eden Valley, and on him. Yet turning his practical proposal into a real marriage means a leap of faith for both…toward a future filled with the promise of love.

COWBOYS
OF
Eden Valley

Available May 2013

LIH82963